OUT OF THE

GAY ROMANCE COLLECTION

PENALTY BOX

GENEVIVE CHAMBLEE

Two minutes in the box or a lifetime out

Hockey player Aidan Lefèvre's professional and personal life is on ice. Recovering from an injury and traded to a new team, Aidan is attempting to prove his viability to his coaches, fans, and teammates. Just when he believes he's succeeded, another accident during the playoffs threatens to unravel all of his progress.

Having relocated away from family and friends, Aidan turns to his extroverted team captain, Christophe Fontenot, whose jovial nature lifts everyone's spirits. But when Aidan discovers his attraction for Christophe changes the meaning of "body checking," Aidan questions more than his hockey skills.

Should he deny what he feels or come out of the "box"?

HOT TREE
PUBLISHING

For information, contact the publisher, Hot Tree Publishing.

WWW.HOTTREEPUBLISHING.COM

EDITING: HOT TREE EDITING
COVER DESIGNER: SOXSATIONAL COVER ART
FARMATTING: RMGRAPHX

ISBN: 978-1-925655-40-7

10 9 8 7 6 5 4 3 2 1

To my dad for teaching me that I can and to CKMC who never stopped believing.

CHAPTER 1

"Eight seconds remaining on the power play for the Civets after Fontenot's boxed for slashing, with 3:16 left in the third period. The Cats are trying to get some offense going as Guillory makes a nice cross-ice pass to rookie, Semien Metoyèr. A force-centering pass through the slot, but nothing doing. Guillory to Fontenot off the bench. Shot fired from the point to behind the net. Becket brings it out, up the ice. Intercepted by Lefèvre. Breakaway shot. Fuselier dives, but it sneaks through, tying it up one-to-one. And the crowd is on their feet in the LeFleur-Calais Arena here in Saint Anne. But now Wolves trainers are rushing to the ice. Fuselier's down, not moving."

Staring at Brandon Fuselier sprawled unmoving on the ice, Aidan Lefèvre's smile from his first goal as a Civet faded. Sweat rained from his hairline and meandered languidly down his temple and clung to the scruffy bristles lining his strong jawbone. A stifling silence replaced the roar of the crowd that had consumed the arena seconds ago and deafened him. His chest tightened, as if his lungs had fused with his ribs.

Not a single twitch from Fuselier. Aidan would have noticed had there been.

Move, dammit!

Nothing.

Medics rushed the ice and applied an immobilizing cervical collar before logrolling Fuselier onto a backboard.

"What?" Aidan asked. Vadium Stepanov, his teammate, had said something, but Aidan was unsure if he hadn't understood because of the Russian's thick accent and poor English—not that Aidan's English was much better—or due to a lack of attentiveness.

"He's going to be okay," Vadium repeated.

"Pray it," Aidan whispered. "He's just a kid."

***

"Go home; shake it off," Rusty, the team's trainer, stated, slapping a hand on Aidan's shoulder. "It's all part of the game."

Game. Aidan grunted. It stopped being a game nine years ago when he forwent a college education, signed on with the juniors as a naïve eighteen-year-old, and spent two years working his way up to the majors. It had stopped being a game when he'd unceremoniously been traded from the Owls after last season due to doubt that he'd bounce back from a shoulder injury. It was his job, just like it was Brandon Fuselier's job and future. But now, because of Aidan's shot, Fuselier was lying in Saint Anne Regional Medical Center with a spinal injury, which could possibly be career-ending. And Rusty wanted to call it a game?

Gathering the last of his gear, he slammed his footlocker shut and lumbered to the parking lot, debating whether to join his teammates at the bar. No one felt like celebrating after the playoffs-eliminating loss in double overtime, but it was traditional to have a drink after the last game. And there it was again: game. How sickening that word had become.

Maybe a stiff drink—or two or four—would do him some good. Or not. He wasn't really part of the Civet tradition, was he? He was back to proving his salt, fighting to be given time on the ice, earning the trust and respect of his teammates. Coming from a different conference, he hardly knew any of them. At least, being in Louisiana, some of them spoke French—granted, a different type of French. But he could have been like Vadium. Then again, his Russian teammates had their own unique clique.

Why not go for a drink? It wasn't like anyone was home waiting for him. Sure, he could catch a red-eye to Quebec for the off-season, but no one was waiting for him there, either. Since his father had died, mother remarried, and siblings had scattered across Canada, it hardly felt like home anymore. Two years ago, he'd sold his condo there after a development company decided to build a strip mall with a private airport down the street, thereby eliminating his physical tie to the city. After he'd sold his home, he'd resorted to living in a rental property owned by his brother.

Tossing his bag in the passenger seat, Aidan sat in his car, pressing his palms to his eyes. Nine years. It had taken him four years before he'd played in his first playoff. He'd several behind him now. And how many did Brandon Fuselier have? How many would he have?

A knock on the window startled him. Christophe grinned at him through the glass. Aidan turned the ignition and lowered the window.

"You know where to go, don't you?" Christophe asked, leaning his forearms against the lowered window.

"*Oui*, but I don't know if I feel up to it."

"Nonsense," Christophe rebutted. "You'll come and laugh at Armstrong's karaoke massacre, watch Hopson try to pick up a woman that's not a blowup, listen to Nicco claim he's a real boy, and get shit-faced with the rest of us pathetic reprobates not going to the finals."

A tiny smile tugged at the corners of Aidan's mouth.

"Come on, pretty boy," Christophe persisted, his eyes twinkling in the parking lot lights.

Coming from anyone else, the nickname would have perturbed Aidan, but Christophe was a special case—calling anyone anything at any time for any reason. Christophe didn't discriminate in attaching names to his teammates. As a general rule, the names stuck.

"You're only saying that because I have all my own teeth."

"I admit, I'm impressed you've played all these years and haven't lost any choppers. Then again, it may be because of that soft conference you used to play in."

"Is there anyone on the team you don't harass?"

"Yeah, the people who give me my way. I like them. Agree, and I'll like you."

"Fine." Aidan caved to the jokester left wing. Good-humored and liked by all, Christophe was a perfect choice for team captain. "But I'm not staying long."

"Everyone says that until Peters starts farting show tunes and the bar owner gives free rounds to make him stop."

Aidan didn't bother suppressing his laughter, and Christophe rose from the window; his blond curls, still damp from showering, slapped across his cheeks.

"You'll have a good time."

"*D'accord.* And if I don't, you're paying my tab."

"Deal."

CHAPTER 2

Aidan lumbered into the tavern off Rue Cognac with the enthusiasm of an insect sprayed with repellent. Stuffing his fists in his pockets, he scanned the expansive room with antique chandeliers and dual-motor fans suspended from exposed cypress beams. An array of photographs, framed jerseys, and art deco artwork adorned the copper-sheathed brick walls. A bit swanky for the standard haunt for hockey players in Aidan's opinion, but no one asked him. He joined a gaggle of his teammates huddled at the end of the long bar.

"Malt Scotch," Christophe ordered for Aidan before Aidan ordered for himself. "Trust me. You'll want to try it."

"Aidan doesn't want that old men's drink," Metoyèr razzed, referring to Christophe being one of the oldest players on the team.

"Hush up over there, junior, before I have them card you," Christophe jawed back. "Your bedtime's in an hour."

"Yeah, well, unlike you, I won't be going alone."

"Au contraire, you'll be going with two hands exactly like me."

Ryan Hopson leaned against the counter. "And you'll both be blind by forty."

"Nonsense," Metoyèr ribbed, "Fontenot's already over sixty."

"The rate Semien whacks off, he'll be blind by twenty," Nicco interjected.

"I'm twenty-two, you turd."

Aidan accepted his Scotch from the bartender and glanced around the room in search of a secluded corner or less lively area. His teammates littered the room, like speckles on an egg. No way would he be able to avoid them. If he waited, perhaps, he could sneak out quietly.

"Hey," Christophe stated, elbowing Aidan, "there's a hot little number at six o'clock checking you out."

Glancing over his shoulder, Aidan observed the curvaceous redhead wearing a black latex dress eyeing him, and pressed his lips together. He didn't want to say she looked like a hooker, but... hooker. He frowned.

"She looks more your type than mine," he replied, turning back toward the group.

An odd silence overtook the group, and Christophe

stared hard at Aidan with a tight and curious smile before shrugging and raising his glass. "Cheers," he stated. "Okay, enough with this retro grunge. It's time for some disco."

Nicco waved to the bartender. "I'm going to require something stronger than beer for this. Your version of the stanky chicken is foul."

"Funky chicken, you moron," Christophe yelled, making his way toward the stage. "Disco is back!"

Aidan looked at Nicco. "Did I say something wrong?"

"Not yet, you haven't." Nicco laughed. "Drink up."

"I know you," the hooker... er... redhead greeted Aidan.

"Probably not."

"I do. You play for the Civets."

"So does he," Aidan replied, grabbing Vadium by the arm as he passed and pushing him toward the woman. "He needs a green card."

"*Kakóŭ*? I have visa."

"American Express, too. You'll need it."

"I don't understand."

"Dance with her," Aidan responded, shoving Vadium forward again.

Nicco chuckled. "Man, how you just going to pass over a scorching piece of ass like that?"

Aidan polished off his Scotch in a long gulp. "I'm not interested."

"Why? I never see you with anyone."

"So? Doesn't mean I have to take the first one that comes along."

"No," Nicco disagreed, snatching his fresh drink from the bar. "There have been others, and you never bite."

"I'm not hungry."

"You someone's side piece?"

Sighing, Aidan recognized Nicco's questions wouldn't cease until he had a more definitive answer. "I'm not looking for a relationship right now."

"Hellfire! Who said anything about a relationship? You've never heard of a hookup?"

"I'm not in the mood, okay?"

"Are you ever?"

Christophe danced through the crowd back to the bar, his hips swaying in a manner that conveyed he knew exactly what to do in bed when not alone. "What are you two jabbering about like a couple of biddies?"

"Why Aidan doesn't have a woman."

"Oh?" Christophe's brow arched. "Why don't you?"

"That's not what we were discussing."

"Yes, it was."

Aidan cracked his neck. "That's what you were discussing. I was leaving."

"Touchy." Hissing, Nicco tossed up his hands. "Someone burned you extra crispy."

Christophe blocked Aidan's exit and waved to the bartender. "Two more Scotches. Don't leave yet, pretty boy. We're up next for karaoke."

Aidan gasped as Christophe's eyes brightened with something Aidan couldn't label—or rather, refused to—and a tremor skidded through him. "I can't sing."

"That's the entire point." Christophe handed Aidan the Scotch. "Drink up so you can blame it on the booze."

Aidan shook his head. "I'm not going up there."

"If you're part of this team, you are. It's tradition."

"Damn all this tradition."

"If Vadium can belt out 'Boogie Shoes,' you can stammer through 'Hot Stuff.'"

Aidan could continue refusing, but what was the point? Christophe would continue making the ridiculous sound sane. It gnawed at Aidan that he needed to work on being more of a team player outside of the rink. He didn't hog the puck, always gave credit to his teammates in interviews, and donated to his teammates' charities when asked. What he didn't do was socialize. Anyway, what was singing one song— besides three humiliating minutes on stage in front of damn near every person he knew in Louisiana, plus some? He guzzled his second Scotch and ordered a third.

CHAPTER 3

Aidan opened his eyes, urgently needing to relieve himself in more ways than one. Rolling from his side to his back, he landed with a thud, both his head and right calf striking a solid object. Pain splintered throughout his body. Squinting, he attempted to bring his dark surroundings into focus and decipher what was happening in his spinning world. A narrow stream of light shone through a window. Okay, he was inside somewhere with shag carpet. Reaching, he felt a soft, solid object to his left. Pillows. Leather. Ah, a couch. To his right, he felt wood, metal, and cool glass. A table. Piecing it together, he determined he was wedged on a floor between a couch and table. But where? He didn't have a table in front of his couch. He fumbled to remember. The last thing he remembered was talking with that loudmouth reporter, Toby Harrelson, from XJJ.

Oh shit! What had he said? Later. Now, he needed to figure out where the hell he was. He maneuvered his twisted limbs to sit erect. A bright light clicked on, and Aidan squeezed his eyes shut.

"You okay there, pretty boy?"

Christophe. Okay. Aidan could rule out being abducted by aliens. Well, maybe not. This was Christophe, after all.

"Why am I on the floor?"

"How the hell should I know?" Christophe chuckled. "I deposited your drunken carcass on my sofa. It must not have suited your Sleep Number needs."

"I feel like roadkill."

"I imagine so, the way you kicked them back."

Slowly, Aidan opened his eyes to view Christophe standing at the edge of the table, all rippling abdomen muscles, golden skin, and powerful thighs, wearing nothing but cotton boxers with a noticeable bulge in the front. It drew Aidan's attention to his own physical state, and he grunted. He'd no time for this type of foolishness at this time of night… morning.

"What time is it?"

"Almost six."

Aidan rolled and sat back on his heels.

"Need some help?"

"I got it," he mumbled, standing. "Bathroom."

"Down the hall, first door on the left."

When Aidan emerged from the bathroom, he followed the sounds of movement to the kitchen, where he found Christophe stirring ingredients in a bowl and transforming the mundane task into something incredibly sensual.

"Coffee's on," Christophe stated, spotting Aidan in the doorway. "I thought I'd make us pancakes."

"You cook?"

"When I want to eat." He pointed with a wooden spoon to a stool positioned at the island. "Have a seat. There's something for your head if you need." He motioned to a glass of water and a bottle of aspirin on the countertop.

"*Merci*," Aidan grumbled, sitting. "So, tell me. How big of a fool did I make of myself?"

Christophe smiled lopsidedly. "Ginormous—just shy of a tabletop striptease."

"Wonderful."

"Naw, I'm teasing. You weren't too bad." He stopped stirring and studied his houseguest. "You don't remember any of it?"

"I think I recall talking to Toby Harrelson."

Christophe burst into a wide grin. "Yeah, you really let that assclown have it… in two languages. I don't think he'll be asking you for another interview soon, especially after you threatened to yank out his hair implants and stuff him and his snazzy orthopedic shoes in your storage bench if he came within fifty yards of you."

Heat coursed up Aidan's neck. "You're joking."

"Nope. Want me to remind you what you said about his cameraman?"

Aidan raised his palm and swallowed two aspirin dry. "Spare me."

"It was fun seeing a not so serious side to you." The batter sizzled on the griddle. "Now you've sunk to the gutter with the rest of us."

"Any word on Fuselier?"

"Nothing more than the initial release of him being evaluated by the doctors." He flipped the pancake. "It wasn't your fault, you know."

"It was my puck."

"Your job. You took the shot. Any of us would have. What do you think you should have done? Just looked at it? No. You try to score, and that's what you did. Into the net. And it's Fuselier's job to block, which he tried but failed. It's no one's fault, Aidan. Just an unfortunate freak accident."

"Maybe."

Christophe placed pancakes on a platter. "There's no maybe about it. At my antiquated old age, I've learned five givens in hockey."

"Which are?"

"One: never call the referee an asinine jackass—at least, not to his face when there's two minutes left on the clock. Two: don't urinate on the rink while it's being frozen. There's plenty of opportunities to add bodily fluids to the ice during regular play, with the added bonus of not being fined. Three: don't substitute golf clubs for hockey sticks. I don't care how good of a bargain you get. Someone is going to notice, and it won't go over well with the league. Four: never, and I mean never, gift the person operating the scoreboard a box of laxatives disguised as chocolates prior to a game—unless, of course, the scoreboard operator happens to be your brother-in-law who still owes you money. And five, shit happens."

Aidan smirked.

The glass sliding door leading from an outside dining patio opened, and a brawny African American man wearing a tank and jogging shorts entered. His broad smile transformed from cheery to edgy in seconds upon seeing Aidan.

"Sorry," the man hedged, staring insolently at Aidan and pausing at the door. "I saw your light. I didn't mean to interrupt."

"Trey, this is Aidan," Christophe introduced. "Aidan, this is my neighbor, Trey."

Aidan recognized Trey as the starting quarterback for the Hounds.

"I'm Christophe's teammate."

Trey nodded in acknowledgment, but not completely affably.

"We're having breakfast." Christophe poured more batter on the griddle. "Join us."

"No thanks. I'm about to start my run. Gotta stay in shape. Spring training starts soon."

Christophe poured three mugs of coffee and distributed them. "They get younger each year, don't they?"

"Man, who you telling?" Trey sipped his coffee. "I caught the last of your game last night. Tough loss. Really rough break for the rookie possibly being paralyzed from the neck down."

Nausea rose in Aidan's stomach and pooled at the base of his throat. His lungs burned with a heaviness that made breathing a chore. Without excusing himself, he raced to the bathroom, kneeled on the cool tile in front of the toilet, and retched. He felt like death; however, death was a too-painless escape.

After an indeterminate amount of time, Christophe rapped on the door, then entered. Wetting a face towel in the sink, he hovered over Aidan.

"You okay?"

"Sorry."

"No need to apologize." He draped the towel across Aidan's neck.

"Did you know about the paralysis?"

"Possible paralysis, and it's one of a thousand speculative rumors. Trey should know better than to repeat it, especially since he's been the object of the rumor mill more than a few times."

"Why didn't you tell me when I asked earlier?"

"Because I have common sense." He patted Aidan's shoulder. "Are you able to stand?"

Aidan straightened from his bent position over the

porcelain bowl, waited for his light-headedness to subside, then stood. Removing the damp towel from his neck, he pressed it against his face. Visions of Fuselier diving toward the flying puck replayed in his mind, as if on automatic loop.

"Hockey doesn't offer many do-overs, and regret is pointless."

"I should get home."

"I'll get dressed and drive you."

"You've done enough already. No need to bother yourself. I'll call a cab."

"I'll drive you," Christophe insisted. "After last night, not many taxi services will be willing to have you as a customer."

Aidan lowered the towel, wondering if he should even ask. "Why?"

"Cabbies generally dislike comments of reporting them to the health department for unsanitary vehicles, as you put it, 'encrusted with a hybrid of SARS and an STD' on a live call-in radio broadcast."

"I didn't."

Christophe smiled sympathetically. "You did, bro. It was after the cabbies outside the bar all refused to drive you to the Cleveland Armpit Sniffing Festival."

"The what?"

"The devil only knows, but you and Nicco were adamant. Let me be the first to say, internet search engines aren't your friend."

"Sounds like I was a real charmer." Aidan lowered

the toilet lid and sat. "I apologize for being such an inconvenience."

"You're not."

Squatting, Christophe placed his palms on Aidan's knees, his green eyes comforting and warm. Unaccustomed to the scrutiny, Aidan shifted and retreated slightly.

"Listen. Why not hang out here for a while—at least until you're feeling better? Take a shower. I grabbed your bag from your car, so you have a change of clothes. And I have an extra toothbrush if you need it. Later, you can talk to your agent about releasing a statement. I'm sure the media is camped on your doorstep."

"I hadn't thought about the media being there."

"Of course not. No one knows you're here, except Trey, and he has no incentive to tell anyone."

Aidan's pulse oddly flittered at Christophe's closeness, his scent. His odd reaction to his teammate puzzled him. He considered, then studied Christophe. "Why are you being so nice to me?"

"Because you allowed me to select all the karaoke songs." He squeezed Aidan's knees, then stood. "Wash your face and have some breakfast. It may make you feel better."

Aidan didn't have much of an appetite. In fact, he didn't have much of anything except self-loathing and a monstrous hangover. But since Christophe had gone to the effort of cooking, Aidan would make an attempt to eat, and not be an ungracious houseguest.

After brushing his teeth and washing his face again, Aidan rejoined Christophe, who had put on a terrycloth robe, at the breakfast bar in the kitchen with its simple lines, stark white beadboard cabinetry, Carrara marble countertops, and gray crackle subway tile. Aidan would have guessed Christophe's taste to be more contemporary, with lots of clutter—the way he arbitrarily dumped his personal belongings at any nearby stall in the locker room.

Christophe tracked Aidan's progress across the room to the stool diagonally from him, his gaze intense and impossible for Aidan to ignore. Again, a peculiar feeling unnerved Aidan. He matched the stare, and within a few seconds, it transformed from intense to an invasive ransacking of his mind. Christophe rolled his lips, wetting them as if about to ask a question, but didn't. Aidan swallowed, then broke the gaze and stared into his coffee as if searching for tea leaves to read.

"You have a nice home."

"Yeah, it isn't too shabby for a bachelor. I almost passed on it."

"Why?"

"I was young and thought it was too much of a commitment."

"What changed your mind?"

"Claire. She needed more space. She's one of my better decisions, too."

Over the season, he'd heard Christophe mention

getting home to Claire or picking her up from somewhere. His brow knitted. All he needed was for Christophe's girlfriend to be pissed off that some drunk had crashed on their couch and puked in the bathroom.

"How long have you two been together?"

"Eleven years."

Aidan whistled. "That's a lengthy stint. You two planning on tying the knot?"

Chuckling, Christophe leaned back in his chair. "Now, that would be bizarre, and I'm pretty sure illegal."

"Illegal? You mean she's an illegal immigrant."

"No, I mean illegal, because she's a bullmastiff."

"Oh." Aidan flushed. "Claire's a woman's name."

"Yeah? She's a bitch."

"I just assumed she was your girlfriend."

"I don't know why, since I'm gay."

Aidan fumbled the mug, and coffee droplets splashed the back of his hand. Heat splayed across his face. "Huh?"

"Gay. You do know what that is, right?"

"Of course, but…. You don't seem…." He stopped before making a fool of himself sober.

"Is it a problem?"

"No, I'm… surprised."

"Why? I've never made a secret of it. Granted, I don't have it branded on my forehead—or any other body parts for that matter. Although, I could have it tattooed on my butt cheek. I've been considering getting another tat for some time. I have a buddy who owns a parlor on Saint Henri, and his work is phenomenal." He cut his pancake with a fork. "I honestly thought you knew."

"Why would I know that? You play hockey, drink beer, bench press three-twenty, and drive a ridiculously expensive sports car."

"Is that your checklist for being hetero?"

"No, I'm just saying."

"Just saying what?"

Aidan fidgeted with his mug. "Hell, I don't know. It made sense in my head."

Christophe tossed his head back, his chest and shoulders shaking with laughter. "You're too cute."

"Cute? Are you flirting with me?" A zap of excitement rushed through his body.

"Are you offended?"

Oui. Maybe. Perhaps he shouldn't have asked the question, because it led to a very questionable path—one that Aidan preferred avoiding. What was the saying about slippery slopes?

"Well... depends on if you're serious." *Huh?*

"And if I am?"

Uh-oh. Did he have an answer? "I'm not cute."

"Ruggedly handsome, then. Is that more to your liking?"

"Er...." Aidan's mind blanked. "It's not about my liking. It's about what you like."

What? That was his voice. What the hell was he saying?

21

"I'm not going to lie. I do like what I see. Does that make you uncomfortable?"

Ben ouais. "Not particularly." Aidan gasped at his own response. Obviously, there existed a severe disconnect between his brain, his mouth, and possibly another body part that he didn't want to bring into the equation.

"You don't seem sure."

"I am." *Liar.*

Christophe dropped his fork with a clink against the plate, stood, then rounded the island to stand beside Aidan. Any ordinary time, the distance would have felt acceptable to Aidan and not like an invasion of personal space. But body heat radiated off Christophe, and Aidan began to sweat. He'd even swear the enamel of his teeth perspired. He needed oxygen, a psychological evaluation, and cold shower—not necessarily in that order.

"Don't say something just because you think I want to hear it."

"But you said it's your preference that people give you what you want," Aidan responded, his voice raspier than usual.

"Yes. And are you going to give me what I want?"

"I'm not gay."

"But you're attracted to me—physically."

"You're funny, smart, cool to hang out with. Who wouldn't be?"

"A straight man." Christophe moved closer.

"But I'm not gay. I would know if I were."

Stepping nearer, Christophe snared Aidan in his gaze, like a moth enmeshed in a spider's web. The pinning stare immobilized Aidan. "Label it anything you like."

"I—"

The words were disrupted by Christophe's lips grazing across Aidan's, the pressure probing but delicate. Soft. Nothing like Aidan had anticipated. Wait. Had he anticipated it? Indeed, he had. But when had those thoughts begun? Did he care? Didn't matter. He wasn't....

Christophe's tongue traced along Aidan's lower lip and sought entry permission as his hand tangled in Aidan's hair, cropped stylishly short, and tugged. The carnality of the kiss stunned Aidan into stillness, except for his cock jerking and straining against denim. A moan escaped him. And did his lip just tremble? Where was his control? He was supposed to have control. That's why he was a forward. That's what he did. His job was to control the puck, to control the play. To control his life. To control what was happening now with Christophe's tongue crammed down his throat and his hand... *maudit*!

Christophe's hand released Aidan's jeans button and slipped inside, his fingertips caressing the hair at the ridge of his pelvis.

That feels so incredible. Control, dammit.

Taking advantage of the two inches and twenty-pound difference between them, Aidan stood and used his muscled torso to push Christophe against the island. *Now who's trapped?* Aidan gloated, unrelenting in his surge of command. But Christophe's intention wasn't to play fair, and he shoved his palm further down Aidan's boxers and curled his fingers around Aidan's girth. Aidan's knees nearly buckled, and he snaked his arm around Christophe for support. The deftness of Christophe's fingers aroused Aidan to the point of pain. To the point of….

"Christophe, I can't…."

"Can't what?"

"Oh, *merde*! I can't hold it. I need to come."

"Then, come for me, pretty boy. Come in my hand."

No. Aidan refused to embarrass himself. He wasn't gay. The only reason he was so turned on was because he hadn't had sex with a woman—with anyone—in months. He and Lori had split over three years ago, and since then, dating hadn't panned out for him. The women he met were either groupies, psychotic, or a combination of both. Most didn't know how to deal with his hectic road schedule. Well, Debra had been a possibility. And now that he reflected, so had Hannah. Angelina. Mary Margaret. Okay, so maybe there had been more in the possibility category than he liked admitting. But something between him and them hadn't clicked, and it had seemed futile to invest the time exploring a relationship that he knew in time would fizzle.

He retreated, his chest heaving as if he'd been skating speed drills. He rubbed his palms on the front of his thighs and ignored the dampness beneath his armpits. Not knowing where to look, his eyes darted around the room to the copper pans above the island, herbs sprouting in terracotta pots on the windowsill, the pattern of the Italian floor tile… anywhere except at Christophe.

"You've never been with a man before, have you?"

"I'm sorry."

"Why?"

"I didn't mean to lead you on."

Christophe raked his fingers through his hair. "Is that what you think you did?" He smiled and returned to his stool. "You're not ready."

"I told you. I'm not—"

"I heard you the first two times. It sounds less convincing each time, too." He pointed to Aidan's plate. "Your pancakes are getting cold."

CHAPTER 4

Aidan stared out the window as Christophe drove him to the tavern to retrieve his car. He gazed at the scenery of cane fields, pecan groves, and plantation homes, and submerged himself in his thoughts. The awkwardness and tension between him and Christophe remained heavy in the air, like a wet smog, and neither spoke unless necessary—Aidan to state he needed to return to his car, and Christophe to agree to drive him.

Why was Christophe being gay bothering him? It shouldn't. It didn't change his personality or how talented a team captain he was. It failed to alter how good of a friend he'd been to Aidan—how he always sought to include him in any team afterhours fraternization or offered words of encouragement when Aidan couldn't mask disappointment on his face. And Aidan certainly was no bigot. He'd not been raised to judge or look down on others. So why did knowing this unsettle him? Sure, he could pretend it didn't, but there was something. However, the *something* seemed not about Christophe at all.

A crane flew low across the bayou, searching for food, and snagging Aidan's attention. Cranes were opportunistic feeders, feasting on whatever was available in their habitat. Had that been what had happened with Aidan? Had he allowed what happened with Christophe to occur because he was so sex deprived that he was drawn to the most available person? That hardly seemed right. But maybe. Why had it felt so…?

Aidan shook the thought from his head as he visually followed the crane across the murky water. How was it able to see anything below the surface in that muck? Cranes were migratory birds. He didn't know why that seemed important, or even why it came to mind. In fact, he didn't know why he was focused on a damn crane anyway. He wasn't an ornithologist. His job was skating around a two-hundred by eighty-five-foot ice rink and whacking a vulcanized three-inch rubber disk with a sixty-inch composite stick into a seventy-two by forty-eight-inch net. It had nothing to do with any flipping birds. And he doubted his post-hockey career résumé would include wildlife conservationist. No, he'd probably become a coach or an agent or a home gym infomercial spokesperson peddling thirty days to a slimmer ass equipment.

Get it together. He was losing it, and the wretched disco music blaring from Christophe's speakers wasn't making the situation any better. Christophe bobbed his head to the beat, his hair gleaming in the morning sunlight like the straw spun into gold by Rumpelstiltskin. The majority of his face was obscured by dark aviator sunglasses that on the average person would look clownish but on Christophe perfectly portrayed his eclectic style of looking put-together without the effort of looking put-together. Christophe just did Christophe, and it always worked—on and off the ice. It was the first thing Aidan had noticed about his teammate.

At the conclusion of his first meeting with the Civets' general manager, the GM had said, "Wait until you meet Christophe." It had been an indication then that Christophe stood a step above the rest. At the moment, Aidan felt light-years behind, his thoughts pinging like a pinball from one irrational idea to another. Pinball earned points each time the metal ball made a connection. Aidan's thoughts hung suspended and went nowhere—or, at least, nowhere he wanted them to go.

Sitting in the car beside Christophe for the last ten minutes, Aidan was nowhere closer to understanding why his pulse raced or dick lurched each time he looked to his left. So, naturally, he faced the right and stared out the car window at the stupid crane.

"Good fishing."

"Huh?" Aidan asked, watching the crane fly behind a row of cypresses.

"All these bayous are fishing honey holes. Lots of big bass and fat cats. You fish?"

"Not really." Not for a long time. He'd been eleven years old the last time. It had been before his coach at the time decided he needed to spend more time practicing, and added morning and weekend practices. The coach must have been right, because look at him now: Mr. Professional Hockey Player.

"You should try it. It's relaxing." Christophe flipped on his signal. "You look like you could use some relaxing."

Truth. Starting with the swelling problem between his thighs.

"I relax."

Christophe nodded with little conviction. "Well, if you ever need to talk, I have two ears, instant messaging, text, real-time face chat, and voice mail."

"Voice mail?"

"Some people prefer talking to machines."

"That's weird."

"We live in an age of technology. Smoke signals are passé. The point is, you have options."

"I'll remember that."

"Incoming call from George," an automated female voice from the car speaker announced.

George? Who the hell is George? Aidan's stomach soured.

"I've been meaning to change that. She sounds like a chipmunk." Christophe pushed a button on the steering wheel with his thumb. "Hey, George. What's up?"

"The flooring's still on backorder. The contractor said maybe next week."

"At this pace, you could have flown to Italy and gotten it yourself."

"Tell me about it. I was hoping we could move Saturday to your place."

"Sure. No problem. Let yourself in if I'm not there when you arrive."

"Thanks, Kit. I'll see you then."

Christophe turned into the parking lot of the tavern and stopped behind Aidan's vehicle. It was sporty but not as flashy as Christophe's, and sans the vanity plates. Aidan hopped out before Christophe could speak again.

"*Merci* for letting me crash last night and for the ride here. I appreciate everything." He dashed to his car in two long strides and peeled it out of the parking lot. He needed air. Lots of it. And space.

"*In today's sporting news, Brandon Fuselier remains in critical condition after attempting to block a shot made by Aidan Lefèvre in the playoff game that eliminated the Civets from competing in the national championship. This is the nineteen-year-old's first season with—*"

Aidan clicked off the radio and slammed on his

brakes at the intersection. An angry horn from the driver he'd almost T-boned blared, followed by an extended hand flipping him the bird—the second useless bird in his life today.

Get your shit together. He pressed his palms to his eye sockets and inhaled deeply. Another car horn blared from behind him, alerting him that he was blocking traffic. To silence the horn, he made a right turn, instantly realizing his error and regretting his decision. Blue lights swirled in his rearview mirror, and he pulled to the curb, swearing beneath his breath.

The middle-aged officer spoke into his radio, then approached cautiously. "Sir," he stated, reaching Aidan's door and studying him judiciously, "you almost caused a collision at the intersection, and now you've turned the wrong way on a one-way street."

"Oui," Aidan admitted. No point disagreeing with the obvious. "I got distracted and missed the sign."

"I will need to see your license."

"Sure." Aidan patted his pockets then froze, remembering his wallet was in his duffle bag. And his duffle was in Christophe's car.

Merde! "I don't have it."

"You don't?" Suspicion laced the office's thick Cajun accent.

"I left it in another car. I just got dropped off." Aidan knew it sounded like a lie, and if he were a police officer, he'd have trouble buying it, too.

"Sir, I'm going to need you to step out of the vehicle

where I can see your hands."

Of course, you do. He'd seen enough episodes of *Cops* and *Cajun Justice* to know how this worked.

The officer directed him to the rear of the car. "Have you been drinking?"

"More than six hours ago."

"Will you consent to a breathalyzer?"

Do I have a choice? Declining meant an automatic trip downtown and a car tow. "Should be fun," he muttered, nodding.

"What's that you say?"

An obnoxiously shiny red sports car parked in front of Aidan's, and Christophe exited. "Excuse me, Officer," he stated, pausing beside Aidan's car, "I can vouch for this man."

The officer stared at Christophe with great interest but minimum alarm.

"Who are you?"

"Christophe Fontenot. Aidan's my teammate."

"Slay 'Em All Christophe Fontenot from the Civets?" The officer beamed, and lost interest in Aidan. "You are amazing. I watched the game last night, and I thought y'all would pull it out."

"Yeah, we did, too."

"My entire family and I are big fans. I've been following you since you first signed. My uncle used to work at the arena and get us tickets whenever he could."

Fan? Yeah, I bet. That was more than a fan smile.

The officer looked as if he would devour Christophe.

"Who's your uncle?"

"Oh, I doubt that you know him. He was only a janitor, but his name is Joseph Poppolero. Everyone calls him—"

"Poppy. How's he doing since he retired?"

"Good."

Good. Great. Hello? Remember me? Standing in the sun is hot. Aidan cleared his throat, annoyed.

The officer turned to face Aidan again, and a recognition flooded across his face. "Oh. You're Aidan Lefèvre. I didn't recognize you out of uniform."

"Am I free to go?" Yes, it was impatient and rude, but Aidan didn't give a hoot.

"Sure, sure. No hard feelings. I was just doing my job." He extended his hand to shake.

"Of course," Aidan replied, accepting the officer's hand and applying more pressure than necessary for a firm shake.

The officer's eyes widened as he looked from his squeezed fingers to Aidan's face.

"*Merci* for understanding," Aidan added, releasing.

The officer stepped back and gave Aidan another once-over before a polite smile returned. "Pay more attention to those signs. Nice meeting you, Mr. Fontenot."

"You too. Tell Poppy I said hello."

Christophe threw up his hand as the officer returned to his squad car and made a U-turn, leaving him and

Aidan on the curb. "I don't think you made a good first impression."

"What are you doing here?" Aidan asked, watching the squad car turn into traffic.

"I was following you. You forgot your bag on the back seat."

"You didn't have to."

"No, but it looks like it's a good thing I did."

Ashamed of his poor behavior, Aidan hung his head and studied his feet. "Merci."

Christophe returned to his car, retrieved the duffle, and handed it to Aidan. A sly smile tugged at his lips. "Here, pretty boy. You better get going to where you're headed."

And that was the problem, wasn't it? Where was he headed?

Besides to insanity.

CHAPTER 5

Aidan gazed out of Lesley's high-rise office window onto the Saint Anne's streets below. From above, all appeared peaceful and ordered. Even slower. He focused on a tow-haired child dawdling behind his mother, his attention distracted by the store windows and the adults carrying plastic cups and pushing buttons on their cell phones who brushed passed him without a glance. The boy smiled and waved at each of them, unaffected by their lack of reciprocation. Had Christophe been like that as a child?

Christophe. Aidan grunted and turned from the window to Lesley, seated behind her large desk in her Saint Anne branch office, rapping her pen against the oak. Luckily—or maybe not so much—she was in town. She wasn't happy with him. And what agent would be after the drunken spectacle he'd caused before going MIA for twenty-four hours? With a notorious, even if not reputable, reporter like Toby Harrelson accusing him of making terroristic threats, the situation compelled a statement. But going in front of a camera wasn't an option. There was blood in the water. He'd be hammered with questions regarding Brandon Fuselier, and Fuselier's camp still remained silent. Of course, Aidan understood the reason. Injuries made owners nervous and reduced contracts.

Lesley made a clicking noise with her tongue. "I expect this type of behavior from some of my other clients, but never you. And you say you don't remember what happened exactly."

A hazy memory formed of flashes from a camera and Toby's voice octaves above the socially acceptable level. He remembered heavy arms, his or someone else's. Being jostled in multiple directions as he moved through a crowd. Blurry faces moving close, then away. A strange smoke in his face that faintly smelled of jasmine. Stumbling into arms. Feeling comforted and protected. His hair stroked gently. Being held. Christophe. Aidan shook.

"I remember Toby being in my face."

"But no recollection of grabbing him by the throat and pushing him into the garbage cans?"

"No." And if he did, he probably wouldn't admit it.

"Well, you can't admit guilt, but you could offer a vague, general apology."

"I'm not apologizing to that creep, even if it is my bad."

Lesley dropped her pen. "I've never known you to be this hard-nosed with the media. What do you want me to do?"

"You're my agent. That's what I pay you for… I think. I still pay you, don't I?"

Lesley grinned. "Yes, and you're making me earn every penny."

"Maybe I should retire."

"What?" Her smile dissipated. "Why would you? Are you having some type of breakdown? A pre-midlife crisis?"

Oui. If she only knew. He scratched his jaw stubble. "Doubtful."

"I know this transition hasn't been the easiest for you."

"I'm not such an egomaniac that I'm sulking about being traded. It blows, but that's what happens when you get injured."

"Ah, I see. This is about Brandon."

"You're not paid to psychoanalyze me."

"I'm paid to do whatever to get you the best deals, and if that means cleaning up your personal life—"

"What do you mean cleaning up my personal life?"

"Well, there are rumors."

"What kind of rumors?"

"About the nature of your friendship with Christophe Fontenot."

"He's my teammate."

"And as long as that's what you want to tell the media, that is what we'll say," Lesley replied, the insistence in her tone difficult to hear without wincing.

Aidan's mouth twisted in scorn. "What the fuck, Lesley?"

Her eyes widened in surprise at such brash language from Aidan. She held her palms towards the ceiling and shook her head. "Well, he's openly gay, and you're single."

"So?"

"Sometimes the looks that pass between you two are...."

"Are what?"

"Honestly, they don't always look *teammate-ish*."

He snatched his sunglasses from the edge of the desk and stormed from the room. "I have to go."

"Aidan—"

Aidan punched the elevator down button with his fist, drawing stares from people passing in the corridors. They edged nearer the opposite wall but said nothing.

CHAPTER 6

Behind the double glass doors, the smell of antiseptic permeated the air. Aidan's footsteps echoed against the sterile floor, warranting stares from the nurses. Or perhaps the echoes and stares were all in his mind. He passed a female intern who flashed him a dapper smile. No, the stares were real and not a delusion. He stopped at a desk shielded by a plexiglass window. A large No Firearms sign was plastered to the window. Geez, what happened to the small No Smoking stickers being stuck in a corner? Did it really require a billboard to notify hospital visitors not to come strapping? Like criminals cared and obeyed a damn sign. Besides, the glass was bulletproof, so who gave a damn if someone shot up the bargain basement chairs in the lobby?

"May, I help you?" a nurse asked through a vented

circular hole cut in the window, isolating her from human physical contact. Her tone was dry and flat.

"I'm here to see Brandon Fuselier."

"Are you family?"

What difference did it make? He was a visitor, and if he lied, she'd be none the wiser.

"No."

"He's only allowed family visitors."

"Then I amend my answer. I'm a distant cousin."

The nurse shook her head. "Nice try."

"Listen, I know you have a job to do, and I promise not to stay long or tell anyone you let me in. But I really need to see him."

"Sorry. If I break the rules for you, I'll have to break them for everyone." She dismissed him by returning her attention to a computer screen and pecking at a circular keyboard.

She wasn't the least bit sorry. Aidan fumed, turning away from the window.

"You're Aidan Lefèvre."

Aidan faced the slender man holding a soft drink and leaning against a waiting room door.

"I'm Billy, Brandon's brother."

"Nice to meet you, Billy. How is he?"

"Breathing." He pointed to the bouquet Aidan held. "Are those for Brandon?"

"Oui." He extended the flowers, but Billy didn't accept.

"They won't allow flowers in the CCU. We've turned

dozens away already. I think his team bankrupted a botanical garden. The gesture is nice, but it makes my mother's home look like a morgue. You understand."

Of course, he did. Billy didn't want them. The question was, did he refuse to accept them due to an overabundance, or because of the giver?

"Sure," Aidan replied, dropping the bouquet to his side. "Tell Brandon I came, okay?"

Billy nodded—or something close to it—and left Aidan with an ambiguous interpretation of what it meant. Rattled, Aidan waited for the elevator doors to close, then leaned against the wall, shutting his eyes and thankful he had the space to himself. Several floors later, the elevator stopped, and the doors opened.

"Hey," Christophe greeted jovially stepping inside and reaching to push the button. He dropped his hand, seeing the garage already had been selected. "I'm surprised to see you. I thought you'd be in Quebec."

"I didn't feel like packing," he confessed, a rawness in his tone.

"Well, you always could hire a personal assistant. A lot of the guys have them."

"Do you?"

"I do. I used an agency to find her. I could give you the number."

Aidan shrugged. Did he want someone organizing and knowing his personal affairs? He already had an agent and an accountant. Not packing his own suitcase seemed pretentious to him.

"Are you following me again?"

"Visiting my nana." The elevator doors opened, and the two exited and began walking toward the parking lot. "There's a bistro down the street that sells the best muffuletta. I was going to stop there for lunch. Care to join me?"

Lunch sounded good. Lunch with Christophe sounded better, although complicated. Christophe hadn't made a production about what had happened—or rather, what hadn't happened—between them. He'd been understanding, perhaps too understanding. He'd driven Aidan to his car, and continued as if nothing had transpired. But occasionally, Aidan would notice a flicker of despondency in Christophe's moss-colored eyes.

Agreeing, the two met at the bistro a short time later and were seated in the outside dining area under an umbrella with a paisley print that reminded Aidan of casino carpeting. After ordering, they resumed their conversation.

"Is your grandmother very sick?"

"She lives in the hospital's nursing home."

"I didn't know the hospital had a nursing home attached."

"Yeah, it's real nice. We tried to keep her home as long as possible, but it got to be too much. Dementia. We moved her about three years ago, and I visit her a couple times a month."

"I'm sure she appreciates that."

"Nah. I used to visit more often, but the nurses asked me not to."

"Why?"

"It agitates her. I'm not that surprised, though. When we were children, she always preferred my sisters to me."

"But still, she's your grandmother. It's not the nurses' place to tell you not to visit."

"They *requested* I not visit as much. And at first, yeah, I was offended. But then I realized, I was visiting more for me than for my nana."

Aidan cocked his brow. "What do you mean?"

"When you care about someone, you do what's in their best interest. If my nana is more comfortable in my absence, then that's how it should be. As long as she's happy and safe, I'm good. I'm not going to love her any less. And if she ever needs or wants me, I'll go." He leveled his gaze on Aidan. "I'm not going anywhere."

"You're very understanding."

"Patience is something learned with age, my friend."

Aidan doubted Christophe still was speaking of his grandmother. "You keep talking like you're a hundred years old."

"Thirty-four is getting there in hockey. I envision a couple more years in the league, but after that, who knows?"

"You sound like you have it all sorted."

"Life's lessons. You live them; you learn." He leaned

forward and propped his chin on his fist. "Don't you think about your future?"

"Apparently not the same way you do."

"Meaning?"

"My future is getting through today and working on tomorrow. Not contemplating something that may happen years from now. Building goals and dreams on possibilities is devastating when fate spits in your face and says 'no way, man.'"

"So, spit back."

Aidan laughed. "You're definitely not a poet."

Christophe flashed his jaw-dropping grin. "In junior high school, I wanted to be a rapper. I called myself Dr. Vanilla C. Snow."

The confession didn't stretch Aidan's imagination. "I can see you prancing around a stage with your pants sagging. So why didn't you go for it?"

"How many gay rappers do you know?"

"That doesn't seem a reason that would stop you. It's not like the world of hockey is much friendlier."

Hunching his shoulders, Christophe leaned back while the waitress placed their orders on the table.

"It hasn't been that bad, believe it or not. Sure, there's always a couple of assholes, but after dealing with my parents' reaction, they were cupcakes."

"They didn't approve, huh?"

"Not exactly. But I think they had more of an issue with me boning my sophomore biology teacher than me being gay."

Aidan bit into his sandwich and mentally rolled his eyes. The act seemed typical for Christophe. "Still, it couldn't have been easy. The players must have ribbed you."

"Guys like that have ego issues, and their personal quandaries have nothing to do with me. They can work that out with their therapists."

"I don't follow."

"Take a guy who has a thing for a woman, and she has a mutual interest. Everything is good. But say he's not interested in her, but she's into him. She becomes a pathetic joke to him, not worthy of his time. Flip it that he's interested in her, but she's not into him. Then he'll call her a stuck-up bitch, because she doesn't see his potential. No matter how it's twisted, it's all about him and his perception of himself. It's no different when another man shows interest. If he's offended, it's because of how he feels about himself, and nothing to do with the interested person."

Biting into his sandwich, Aidan chewed slowly, allowing the logic to process. Christophe made sense, more sense than Aidan expected.

"Besides, mediocrity doesn't snag my interest. I only go for prime quality, which eliminates most of the hockey players I know."

Aidan's head snapped up at the lusty playfulness in Christophe's voice, and something in his belly leapt. Direct flirtation. His cheeks stained with color. *Okay, calm yourself. He's not one to play with.*

"You're blushing. How cute," Christophe commented, in the same flirty tone.

Aidan looked away to shield his response to the sensual effect Christophe's voice had on him. "I told you, I'm not cute. Fuzzy dice are cute."

"Especially when hanging from a long pole."

Aidan parted his lips to rebut the coquettish innuendo, but had nothing. He laughed instead. "I walked straight into that one."

"Yeah, you did." Christophe squeezed lemon in his tea, stirred with his finger, then sucked the tip.

Damn, it's hot out here. Grabbing the dessert menu stuck between the ketchup and mustard bottles, Aidan used the stiff cardboard as a fan. It failed to cool him. How could it with Christophe staring at him as if he might pounce at any second? And if anyone knew how fast Christophe could move, it was Aidan. He'd chased him around the rink enough times during drills to not be fooled that his bulky size would slow him. The small circular table between them was not much taller than boards. Christophe could be across it in a single vault.

"Mr. Fontenot," a tiny voice stated from behind Christophe.

Both Aidan and Christophe turned to face a skinny boy standing in front of a tall, slender man who looked to be an older double. Aidan was very appreciative of the interruption.

"May I have your autograph?" the boy asked nervously.

"Of course." Christophe grinned, wiping his mouth and hands with a napkin. "Who am I making this out to?"

The boy stared, confused—or in awe.

"Tell Mr. Fontenot your name," the man prompted.

"Jonathan."

"Jonathan," Christophe repeated, nodding. "That's a good strong name. I have a brother named Jonathan. You remind me of him when he was your age. Do you play hockey?"

"Yes, sir. I want to be like you when I grow up, but I'm not good. I have to sit on the bench."

"That's better than being in the penalty box like some people." Christophe raised his right hand and pointed his left index finger into his palm to indicate Aidan.

The boy beamed, displaying missing front teeth. "But Mr. Lefèvre has the most assists in the league."

Aidan smiled smugly at Christophe. "There, take that!"

"Yeah, yeah," Christophe teased, scrawling his name on the paper. "I bet when you grow up, Jonathan, you'll have just as many or more. But you have to work hard, practice every day, and listen to your coach." He handed Jonathan the autograph.

"Yes, sir." The boy looked at Aidan. "May I have yours, too?"

"Anyone who knows my stats, you bet can have my signature." He signed the paper with a small message of encouragement.

After a few more minutes of chitchat, father and son returned to their table, and the teammates finished their lunch over causal conversation before settling the bill and taking a streetcar to the town square littered with antique shops, vintage clothing boutiques, perfumeries, chocolatiers, fine dining restaurants, and of course, drinking establishments. Strolling the wide sidewalks paved with uniform slabs of slate, they viewed the eye-catching window displays like tourists—which, in many ways, Aidan was. Since moving to Saint Anne, he'd not taken in much of the city other than the shops surrounding the arena, a local dollar store, and the laundromat with paid folding service. He'd been meaning to get out more.

They purchased fresh beignets, then settled on a bench and watched the street performers—break-dancers who spent equally as much time obnoxiously heckling passing pedestrians as they did dancing. For Aidan, the performers were more annoying than entertaining, with their subpar dancing skills, but they were an adequate distraction from the whirl of flummoxing and provoking emotions that occurred each time he glanced in Christophe's direction.

He liked women. He always dated women. He slept with women. Never once had he fantasized about a man. Sure, he felt drawn to Christophe, but that was friendship... the camaraderie of teammates. Explaining Christophe's tongue tangling with his own and eliciting animalistic lascivious desires—well, that remained thorny. But in time, perhaps, maybe, Aidan would formulate an acceptable answer that didn't involve sexuality. Besides, he was beyond the age of sexual exploration and discovery.

He lifted his face toward the sky, allowing the rays of the sun to warm him while it lasted. To the west, dark clouds stacked, indicating another spring shower typical of Louisiana soon on the way. They always began the same way, with heavy droplets, rolling thunder, and disruptive wind that transitioned to a steady, nearly soundless, spray. Fortunately, there were plenty of places he could duck into to wait out a downpour if need be. Or he could leave now and return home to nap. Rain always made a perfect backdrop for sleeping. It would be nice to curl between the cotton sheets on his king-size bed and cuddle with—

"Hey," Christophe stated, elbowing him. "What's that look all about?"

"Huh?"

"You just went from grinning like a kid with a triple ice-cream cone to brooding like a toddler with a soiled diaper."

"It's nothing. But speaking of kids… you're good with them. Ever thought about starting a family?"

"That would be hard, considering."

"From what I've read, the laws have made adoption for same-sex couples easier."

"*Couples,* not singles."

"Why are you single?"

Christophe's eyes flickered again with a knowledge that unnerved Aidan. "You asking about my love life?"

"Sorry. I didn't mean to pry."

"No, I don't mind," he replied, his smile wicked and curious. "My ex and I broke up a year ago. We tried to make it work, but he was too insecure, always trying to one-up everyone."

"How so?"

"Like if you said you came in third in a marathon, he'd say he came in first in a triathlon. He always was bragging about what he had or what he'd done. Last Fourth, mutual friends invited us to a cookout. Everyone was dressed in shorts and T-shirts. He wore pleated trousers and a tie. Then Natalie, the hostess, recently had lost her grandmother and was sharing memories. So, naturally, he starts talking about losing his mother. That was fifteen years ago, and he'd stopped speaking to her—his choice, not hers—five years prior to that." He shook his head in disgust. "I couldn't invest any more of my time in a person like that."

Nodding, Aidan agreed. "That would get on my nerves, too."

Licking sugar from his fingers, Christophe regarded one of the performers promoting a video of their life story for sale. "Maybe I'll do that."

"Do what? Break-dance?"

"Write an autobiography."

Aidan chuckled. "I don't know if the world is ready

to read all your naughty secrets and tales of hockey mayhem."

"That's reserved for pillow talk, but it's a cool title. I may snag it."

"It's all yours."

Pressing his lips together, Christophe made a soft sound. "Ah, giving me what I want again. I knew I liked you."

Thunder grumbled in the distance, still miles away—the clouds not yet having overtaken the sunshine. The lure for an afternoon nap increased, but Aidan enjoyed Christophe's company. In fact, if he were honest with himself, he'd admit that Christophe's companionship was far superior to anyone else's.

"Hmm."

"Hmm what?" Aidan asked.

"There's that look again, like you have a serious thought but can't decide."

"Well, I guess not everyone masters being as poker neutral as you."

"I'm not neutral. You just don't pay attention."

"Maybe I don't want to hear it."

Aidan stood and eased through the audience, down the concrete seating. One of the performers began to heckle him for leaving, but quickly reconsidered after viewing Aidan's dark expression—and his stacks of muscles that could deliver a significant punch. Frequently, other players and male rivals underestimated his strength based on his runway model looks of a strong jawline, eyes the color of the Mediterranean at dusk, and honey-brown hair with streaks of chestnut and auburn, as if it couldn't decide on a permanent color. He was, as Christophe adeptly nicknamed him, a pretty boy, and only the beard stubble he usually sported fractured his beauty to add a rugged edge. But on the ice, outfitted in his bulky pads and uniform, sportscasters described him as a hockey demigod—tall, lithe, and lethal.

Aidan turned to Christophe, who'd caught up with him on the pavement a few yards from the dancers, with apologetic eyes for his abruptness in leaving.

"I'm not going to push you into something you don't want," Christophe stated. "It's not a conversion, either, where you're brainwashed into being a different person."

"I don't know what I want."

"Yeah, you do, but you may be afraid to admit it."

"Were you?"

"A little at first. I was thirteen, at summer camp, and I got a boner every time the assistant instructor came around. He was nineteen and played on a college team. At first I thought I was impressed with his skills— which I was—and that my stiff dick was a combo of groupie admiration and adolescent lack of control."

"What made you think otherwise?"

"That fall, I got my first girlfriend. Normal teenage first-love stuff, only I was far from attracted. She was pretty and funny, but I wasn't interested in holding her hand or trying to feel her up. When I started whacking off, I'd think about her and stroke and stroke. Nothing. Then I'd think about the assistant. Boom!" He tossed the wadded wax paper from the beignet in a trash bin. "I ignored it for a couple more years, until I went to a dark room party."

"A what?"

"It's an abandoned house, usually foreclosed by the bank and not in close proximity to other homes, that kids trashed by spraying graffiti on the walls and naming each room. The dark room wouldn't have a good light source, only a few candles—enough to navigate your way in. Anything goes."

They crossed to the streetcar stop.

"As I walked through, someone grabbed me from behind and began groping me. From the grip and cologne, I knew it was a guy. He didn't say anything, just pushed me against a wall and… well, you get the picture."

A harsh edge laced Aidan's voice, but not one of judgment or disdain. "Just like that? You let him?"

"We've all engaged in spontaneous indiscretions at one time or another."

"No." Aidan's expression twisted, and he gritted his teeth.

Taken aback, Christophe studied his teammate, and gaped at the revelation. "Are you jealous?"

"Why would I be jealous?"

Oui, why would he be because years ago some

random guy ran his hands all over Christophe's hard body and had wild sex with him? Being jealous would make no sense—which didn't explain why he felt pissed off now.

"It's shocking, okay?"

Christophe grinned, unconvinced. "Okay, pretty boy."

The streetcar arrived, and the two rode in silence to Rue D'Iberville where the most prestigious hotels of the city lined both sides of the brick street. Not much of a crowd walked the sidewalks, possibly due to the threat of rain dissuading the tourists from leaving their hotel rooms. Aidan looked up at Le Château Elysian towering above him and considered. When he'd left this morning, the media still had been lingering around his front yard, and he imagined some remained. Once the media caught scent of a story, they didn't shake easily.

"Think they'll let me have a room without a reservation?"

"If you tell them to pick a platinum card, they will." Christophe shifted. "If the media's still bothering you, you're welcome to crash at my place. Claire's going to be at the vet's a few more days, so I could use the company."

"You didn't mention anything being wrong with Claire."

"She had hip surgery a few days ago, and the vet is keeping her to ensure she stays immobile. The offer stands."

"*Merci.* No offense, but I thought I spotted an alligator in your backyard."

Christophe laughed in a deep, rich baritone. "You did. That's Allie."

"You have a pet alligator?"

"She's mechanical. I bought her from a Hollywood prop shop few years back as a deterrent when I was having issues with paparazzi hopping my fence. She works on a timer and moves to different locations in the yard. She also has a motion sensor and snaps."

"Clever."

"In this business, you have to be."

Aidan hooked his thumbs in the front pockets of his jeans. "I think," he stated, staring at the pavement, "I want to go inside."

"Okay, but if you change your mind, you know where I am."

Christophe pivoted, but Aidan caught him by the elbow.

"I want you to come inside with me."

"You sure?"

Aidan nodded, more confident than hesitant, but not completely assured.

"Tell you what," Christopher suggested, "you get a drink at the bar, and I'll get the room and meet you."

CHAPTER 7

Le Château Elysian was as impressive on the inside as it was on the outside—from the brass door opened by doormen dressed in waistcoats, to commissioned artwork by contemporary artists adorning the walls, to the arched ceiling with carved crown molding. It wasn't the type of hotel he generally stayed in, although the league typically booked nice establishments when on the road.

Aidan ordered a rum and Coke from the bar, but fiddled with the glass more than drank. A lump formed in his throat, and his skin prickled as if bitten by nightcrawlers. What on earth was he doing? He resolved to change his mind, but seeing Christophe twirling the card key made him catch his breath, and his pulse rate rose. With a flick of his wrist, he swirled the liquor in the tumbler, held it for a moment while it stilled, and inhaled the bouquet.

Sensing Aidan's continued wavering, Christophe settled at the bar beside him. "No pressure," he assured, staring at their reflection in the mirror behind the rows of premium liquors. With his palm flat on the counter, he caressed the side of Aidan's hand with his pinky finger.

Aidan's fortitude returned. After downing his drink in one swallow, he trailed Christophe to the elevators and then to the suite on the ninth floor. He hesitated at the door, unsure if he needed to remove his shoes before stepping onto the Persian rug that covered a good portion of the polished walnut floor.

"Posh," he stated.

"I'll say. But I figured if you were going to be holed up here a while, you'd want something homey."

Aidan turned in a small circle. "My place looks nothing like this. In fact, it's just a one-bedroom bungalow at the end of *Le Quartier Jardin*." When he completed his circle, he unexpectedly came face-to-face with Christophe, who had stepped closer.

Neither moved, yet both searched for unspoken answers. Their tangled breathing thundered in his ears.

Like a virgin on a wedding night, Aidan stood dumbfounded and uncertain of how to approach, and what was expected. Therefore, he equated it to the only thing he knew and executed well: hockey—his comfort zone.

When he was learning to play hockey, the first thing he learned, aside from how to tape his stick, was to have a plan. Currently, with Christophe, he had no viable plan. It may be Aidan's first time but damn if he wanted to look like a rookie with his knees knocking and pits saturated. In a faceoff—similar to his current situation—the aim was twofold—anticipate what his opponent would do and keep his eye on the puck. In this case, he needed to anticipate what Christophe— his soon-to-be lover—wanted him to do. Stick hand position—a pun if ever there was one—often was the critical telltale sign of an opponent's intentions. Christophe's hand hung unmoving by his side, letting Aidan make the first move and freely choose—making good on his word of no pressure. It was an open-net shot, a forward's dream.

While Aidan appreciated the offering of space and acknowledgment of free will, part of him wished Christophe would take what he wanted—at least, to start. *Charge the net, Christophe.* But no, Christophe wouldn't do that, Aidan recalled, because Christophe preferred people to *give* him what he wanted instead of taking it.

The second part of the strategy was to maintain eye contact with the puck, the object of desire. And oh, what an object to desire Christophe was. Admiring, as well as considering, Aidan took in the six-foot-one mass of muscle before him. Physically, he was attracted—a first. Everything about Christophe stirred something in him. Christophe's green eyes remained focused and daring, his nose straight except for a small lump where it had been broken and repaired a time or two. His cheekbones were high, and he had tanned olive skin. This, Aidan's target—his puck—awaited the play, the drop. As a center, Christophe had had a 53.3 percent faceoff win rate before moving to left wing—a move Aidan didn't understand. But that had occurred years before he'd joined the Civets. Centers could change the course of play within seconds. But Christophe maintained restraint.

Continuing his scrutiny, Aidan lowered his observation to Christophe's strong lips that easily could have been cut from a statue. Unconsciously, Aidan traced his thumb across Christophe's lips. When Christophe drew in the thumb and sucked lightly, Aidan felt an uncomfortable tightness between his thighs, and a tingle of electricity radiated throughout his body.

Damn, that's hot.

Sensing the increased arousal, Christophe took more of Aidan's thumb but maintained eye contact. He pulled off slowly and allowed it to pop out of his mouth. *Tease.*

Encouraged, Aidan raked his lips across Christophe's, the fire inside him igniting. In response, Christophe tilted his head, offering more of his mouth and fielding no resistance. Increasing aggression, Aidan nipped at Christophe's lower lip, his kiss both demanding and possessive. Christophe's response matched.

This felt right. Natural. In no way would Aidan be discouraged now. He explored Christophe's mouth—tongue, teeth, lips—taking, giving, wanting, and generating *mouthgasms*. His body felt defiant of gravity, suspended in a cloud of emotions. Christophe's lips, firm yet tender, awoke every atom of arousal.

"So good," Christophe murmured. "More."

Who was Aidan to refuse? Placing his hand behind Christophe's neck, he pulled him closer. His other hand snaked behind Christophe's waist and dipped beneath his shirt, massaging the small of his back. The connection of flesh vaulted both to the next level.

Momentarily, Aidan became twisted in his shirt as he attempted to tug it over his head, helpless as Christophe raked his nails across his broad clavicle, over his stone-hard nipples, down his flat stomach, and skimmed the strip of dark hair from his navel to his jeans. Zipper down, Christophe shoved the denim to Aidan's ankles, along with his boxers. Freeing himself, Aidan tugged at Christophe's garments. A frenzy of fabric drifted in the air. Shirts, shoes, and pants flew in various directions, landing across chairs, over lamps, and on the floor.

Aidan had seen plenty of nude men before in the locker rooms and showers, but never previously had he viewed one as he observed Christophe—tall perfection, a replication of Adonis or Hercules. Beautiful. Solid, smooth pectorals. Flat, stacked six-pack abs. Sculpted quadriceps. The nest of curls a shade darker than his gold tresses above a thick nine inches of pleasure. Aidan ogled Christophe—inspected each individual inch—and became self-conscious. He pulled away. However, Christophe's voice made any embarrassment evaporate.

"I want," Christophe huffed, dropping to his knees, his eyes indicating his lustful intent. He kneaded Aidan's thighs, sending an electrical sensation throughout Aidan's body before wrapping his devilishly talented fingers around the base of Aidan's cock and licking the tender head made shiny from leaking fluid. "My pretty boy."

"I—" He was interrupted by Christophe's lips encircling him. The guttural groan Aidan released sounded beastly, and his hips bucked forward.

Not deterred by Aidan's impatience, Christophe continued at the same pace, taking more in at each suck and adding more pressure with each pull of the rigid flesh. With a firm grip, he jerked the shaft in quick yanks while he vigorously tongued the head. It was as if Christophe sensed how much Aidan could withstand without going over the edge, and he aroused him to the brink.

Aidan watched, as much turned on by the view as the sensation. "Incroyable," he yelped, placing his palms on Christophe's shoulder and shoving in earnest. His need built quickly. "I'm close," he panted, the words barely audible.

With the confession, Aidan saw Christophe's cock

twinge, and Christophe began fondling his own balls like worry stones. It was the second sexiest act Aidan had ever witnessed—the first being the way Christophe relaxed his throat and accepted all of him with ease.

"*Oh, mon Dieu,*" Aidan groaned, digging his fingers into Christophe's flesh. His body shuddered as he released, and he lost himself in desire. His heart thumped against his chest with each jet.

Christophe looked upward, his lips glistening with semen and a hunger still in his eyes. "You sound so sexy when you come."

"What about you?" Slipping his hands under Christophe's arms, he urged him to stand. "You didn't finish."

"That's okay."

"But I want you satisfied, too." He stroked Christophe's cock that stood flat against his pelvis.

"Well, I'm not going to argue." Christophe grinned. "What did you have in mind?"

"What do you like?"

"I like it all."

"Then what is it that you want?"

He pressed close to Aidan and whispered in his ear. "To bend you over and fuck you like the world is going to end."

"Okay."

Christophe tensed briefly. "Aidan, it's intense. You need to be sure."

He kissed Christophe's lips, tasting the salt of his

own seed. "I am."

Taking his hand, Christophe led him to the bedroom, pausing to retrieve two foil packets from his discarded trousers. Using his teeth, he tore open the foil, then rolled on a condom, and situated Aidan on the mattress on all fours. Stepping behind him, he rubbed his hands from Aidan's shoulders to hips in circular strokes. He paused again to open the second foil packet, and squirted the cool lubricant on Aidan's rear.

"Are you always so prepared?"

"I'm not a monk, if that's what you mean," Christophe answered. "But no, it's not an everyday occurrence."

With quick but easy strokes, Christophe worked in the lubricant. The insertion of Christophe's long finger caused Aidan's breath to hitch in panic. "Breathe," he soothed, inserting a second finger to the knuckle. Obediently, Aidan complied, and the ring of muscle relaxed. "That's right, pretty boy. I have you." After working Aidan's hole with several hard probes, Christophe positioned his cock against the opening and began to glide in.

Aidan exhaled a shaky breath, both in delight and the pain of being stretched as Christophe filled him to capacity. It burned and sparked simultaneously, and Aidan gripped the sheets reflexively. Christophe's thrust brought a sweet pleasure and rubbed all the right places. Aidan's cock hardened again at the movement.

Christophe's assault began slow and methodical

and rapidly transformed into an intense lightning exhibition as he wasted no time building speed. Each thrust was harder and deeper than the previous, searching for the maximum depth and desiring to leave no area untouched as if he was marking his territory to set a standard too high for anyone to follow.

Aidan locked his elbows to prevent from tumbling face-first into the mattress from the pounding. Surely, he'd be sore afterwards, but damn, it felt good. Christophe struck his prostate with precision and accuracy, the way he would slam a puck into an undefended net. At every pass, his body surged. Sweat rolled from his temples onto his cheeks.

Hooking his arms beneath Aidan, Christophe clasped his hands on Aidan's shoulders, drawing him in for each plunge. He uncoiled in rapid, savage thrusts that stripped Aidan of strength to form coherent thoughts. And from the garbled, throaty grunts Christophe made, Aidan imagined his thoughts blurred with pleasure as well. Fireworks exploded in Aidan's anus, clamping the cavity tight around Christophe in a compressed sheath. Christophe responded to the constriction with a diminished self-control into nothing, reduced to ragged pants and feral gasps, and heat. Seconds later he erupted buried inside Aidan. Hearing Christophe's raw cry, Aidan exploded, splashing his chest and dripping onto the sheets.

Breathless, they both collapsed onto the bed.

"Wow," Christophe gasped, shoving his hair from

his eyes in his post-orgasmic haze.

Aidan nodded. That summed it up perfectly.

CHAPTER 8

Rain pelting against the window woke Aidan a short time later. He didn't recall climbing beneath the thick duvet or falling asleep, but he was warm, snug, and being held by strong arms. Familiar arms. And, he realized, the smile plastered on his face wasn't the result of a dream.

"Hey," Christophe said, stroking his cheek.

"How long was I asleep?"

"Not long. Anyone ever tell you, you talk in your sleep?"

"No," he admitted alarmed. "What did I say?"

"Let's just say I'm flattered."

Aidan groaned. He could imagine. "Egads."

Christophe laughed. "You're so sexy when you blush."

Rolling on his back, Aidan scooted to a sitting position and flinched at a stab of pain in his rear. He adjusted to bear more of the weight on his hip.

"You okay?"

"Oui."

Contrition streaked across Christophe's face. "I shouldn't have taken you so fast."

Aidan smirked. "If you could do it again, you'd do it the same—hard, fast, and with abandon."

Wincing, Christophe studied him. "No abandoning."

"Huh?"

"Aidan, I wasn't looking for a hookup. I can get that anywhere. I was looking for something more... steady."

"How steady?"

"I don't mean marriage; at least, not tomorrow. I have an endorsement interview, and there's no way I'd be able to find a dress in time. But seriously... a relationship."

"Oh."

"That isn't encouraging."

"This is all new. I don't know if I want to...."

"To what?"

"Put it out there." His brow knitted. "Say that I'm...." He shook his head. "My family...."

"I'm not asking you to come out of the walk-in. Some of them are quite roomy. That's for you to decide. I'm talking about us, if there is an *us*." He sighed. "I probably should have mentioned it before we had this amazing afternoon, indulging in the lustful desires of the flesh."

Aidan chuckled. "Still not a poet, but yes, it was amazing."

"Was? Past tense?"

"I'm not good at relationships."

"Have you tried? And I don't mean the only criteria being remembering her birthday. Mine is August ninth, by the way."

"Of course, I have."

"And what's the longest one you've had?"

He hunched his shoulders. "*Je ne sais pas*. A couple of months."

"A couple of...?" Christophe allowed the question to die on his lips. "Have you ever considered that they haven't lasted because none have ever been with the right person—or a dashing left wing with excellent taste in Scotch."

"I guess that's a possibility." He shifted his weight again and grinned. "How does anyone have a serious conversation with you?"

"I don't generally have any serious conversations while naked and in bed, but for you, I'm making an exception." He leaned and kissed him tenderly.

Aidan's body responded as warmth spread to his extremities. "Can we keep *us* between us?"

"I told you before, pretty boy, I never advertise my private business. As long as there *is* an *us*, there can be a just us."

Aidan slid his hand across Christophe's thigh and groped his engorged cock. It was smooth and warm beneath his touch. Slowly, Aidan skidded his hand up and down the shaft until he saw clear liquid bead at the slit. He rubbed his thumb across the thick, dark head and licked his lips.

"I want to, but I don't know how."

"Lucky for you, I'm willing to be both your personal trainer and guinea pig. But you may require lots of lessons." He wiggled his eyebrows. "Do what you think feels good."

Nodding, Aidan lapped at the head like it was an ice-cream cone, swirling his tongue over, around, and across repeatedly before skimming along the thick vein to his testicles and sucking them in one at a time until Christophe grunted. Then simultaneously until the swollen balls pulsated against Aidan's mouth.

Adrenaline flooded Aidan as he grew bolder and more confident. The delicious texture of Christophe's skin thrilled him, and he took more of him. He allowed Christophe's aroused cock to bump his throat and used his hand to spread the wetness down the remainder of the shaft he was unable to take.

"Holy fuck," Christophe gasped, his voice gravelly and raspy. Aidan had never heard Christophe sound this way but recognized it as one of a man teetering on the edge.

Aidan sealed his jaws, intensifying the suction, and pulled hard. The sweet, salty tinge of precum dispersed across his palate. Using the flat of his tongue, Aidan vigorously swept around the sensitive rim.

The act destroyed Christophe. His seed poured out of him, trickling down Aidan's throat. Aidan surprised himself by swallowing the load, lapping heartily at any spilt droplets.

"Look at you, sucking down my cum," Christophe murmured, after the last orgasmic wave passed. "A-plus to my star student."

For a long while, they lay entwined in each other's embrace, listening to nature's lullaby, and sampling each other's delectable kisses. Then a thought occurred to Aidan.

"Are you really planning on wearing a dress to your wedding?"

Christophe whacked him with a pillow.

CHAPTER 9

"Four days after the Wolves' triumphant double overtime victory, eliminating the Civets from the playoffs, there is still no word on rookie goalie, Brandon Fuselier. Fuselier was carried from the ice and transported to Saint Anne's Regional, where he remains in intensive care. Sources close to the family report Fuselier has not regained consciousness since being injured. Fuselier suffered the injury attempting to block a goal by Aidan Lefèvre that tied the game one-to-one with seconds remaining in the third. Game footage indicates that Fuselier may have been struck by the puck, and that the shot may have been aimed intentionally at the goalie's head; although, no official word has been given on the matter. League officials state the incident remains under review. Sources close

to Fuselier allege bad blood between Fuselier and Lefèvre after Lefèvre was traded from the Owls last season. A scuffle with Brody Simmons, Fuselier's half brother and defensive man for the California Musk-Oxen, and Lefèvre last season resulted in Lefèvre being sent to the penalty box and the Musk-Oxen scoring the winning goal on the power play. Lefèvre later left the game with a shoulder injury, reportedly stemming from the incident, that kept him benched for much of the season. Lefèvre's injury has been rumored as being one of the reasons, along with his underperformance during the regular season, for his trade from the Owls to the Civets. Sources contend Lefèvre has stated he holds Simmons responsible for this series of events and that the discord between Lefèvre and Simmons has seeped over to create tension with other members of Simmons' family, including Fuselier. After the recent game between the Civets and Wolves, Lefèvre was accused of hitting a reporter in a drunken rage, later stopped by city authorities for reckless driving, and has gone into seclusion—"

"What?" Aidan spat. Bile rose in the rear of his throat, and he struggled to gulp it back.

Christophe clicked off the television and set the remote on the console. "Don't pay that report any mind. It's garbage."

"He said I had a grudge for Fuselier. People listen to this. They'll believe it."

"People believe in the tooth fairy and Easter Bunny,

too; although, that tooth fairy is a cheap bitch. She never left me more than a nickel, and nothing past the age of twelve when I've lost the most teeth."

Aidan reached for his phone.

"Who are you calling?"

"My agent. She's supposed to be taking care of this. This doesn't look taken care of."

"No one is going to believe this. It makes zero sense."

"He's a kid. I wouldn't harm a kid, especially not intentionally."

Christophe plucked the phone from Aidan's hand. "You're getting all worked up over nothing."

"It isn't nothing. I'm not stupid. Being unconscious for four days is serious. It can mean brain damage." He snatched the phone back.

"If it's true. Anytime the media proclaim 'sources close to,' expect a lie from some inbred, eleventh or twelfth cousin twice removed with a tombstone tooth, pinwheel plastic eye, residual hemorrhoids, and who hasn't seen the person since kindergarten."

"Easy for you to not be concerned. It's not your career being trashed. You're cozy with your million-dollar franchise endorsements." Aidan regretted the words before completing the sentence.

Christophe's stare grew cold. "You have a problem with my endorsements?"

"No, I'm just—"

"Overreacting to a fabricated media broadcast from

a bogus station that has the morality of a wasted meth head and the honesty of a generational politician."

"And viewership of seven-point-five million."

"Seven million who probably live in the remote corners of the Dominican Republic and don't give a rat's ass about hockey, and the other point five who are asleep, which is what you should be this time of morning… what I should be."

"No one's keeping you up."

Christophe glanced at his crotch. "No?"

"You're insatiable."

"I don't recall that ever having been a complaint."

"No one's complaining." He put a bit more distance between them, placing his hand on Christophe's chest with the intention of pushing him away. The solid firmness wouldn't bulge. "But you're minimizing the situation by distracting me."

"I'm a distraction?"

Aidan nodded toward Christophe's groin. "That is, *oui*."

Sitting against the pillows, Christophe laced his hands behind his head. "Fine. Call your agent at two o'clock in the morning and see how well that goes over. While you're at it, invite everyone up here for a pajama press conference to deny it all."

"They are saying," he hissed, slapping the back of his hand into his palm for emphasis, "I *intentionally* tried to end his career."

"No one will believe that."

"His family does."

"They say that?"

"His brother all but shoved me out the waiting room window to get me gone."

Christophe scrunched his face. "That doesn't make sense."

"It makes perfect sense if they believe it."

Furrowing his brow further and pursing his lips, Christophe shook his head, unconvinced. "Brandon's from a hockey family." Dragging his fingers across Aidan's neck, Christophe speared his digits through Aidan's hair "You want my opinion, the less fuss, the quicker it's dispersed. Let the media show all their cards and have nothing left to spin."

"Except everyone will remember the lies and not the truth."

"It was a good shot. What people will remember is the goal. They may even remember the bullshit boarding penalty I got called for."

While Aidan had confidence in Christophe's conviction, he still felt abandoned in support. However, he dropped it, because continuing the yin-yang debate got him nowhere. Christophe's position was secure. Bad press would make little difference to him. Aidan, with doubt still lingering about his recovery, had more reasons to avoid a negative public image. Plus, he wasn't so low of a cad he'd engage in such callous behavior, although.... He hadn't hit Toby Harrelson, he didn't think, but he should have. In fact, he should have slugged him into next week.

Aidan squirmed beneath the blanket, warming himself. If he knew how to work the thermostat, he would have adjusted the temperature. But being cold provided an excuse to allow Christophe to run his hands across him—something still not wrapped around Aidan's brain. He had a lover. A *male* lover.

Closing his eyes, he decided to deal with it all later.

CHAPTER 10

Emotions were tricky, and Aidan's emotions now were no different. As he watched Christophe leave for his day's appointments, Aidan felt the uncertainty about the night's events creeping into the more conscious portions of his brain. He could have said something to Christophe about what he was feeling, but he smiled and told him he'd call him later—a standard line he'd often used and rarely made good on. If Christophe felt Aidan's wavering, he didn't say, but the look he cast before exiting indicated that he might. Aidan waited only a few minutes after the door closed before booking a flight to Quebec.

***

Aidan hated flying, and his flight had been riddled

with turbulence the entire six hours. Even when he changed planes in New York, his body felt as if it still were being bobbled and jolted. Nerves rattled, he'd had several drinks in the airport bar in addition to the ones on the plane. If he was honest with himself, the flight conditions weren't the only reason for his jangled nerves or alcohol consumption.

He paid the taxi driver, and wheeled his suitcase around the brownstone to the backyard and knocked on the red-painted door before opening it without awaiting a response. His mother's home was modest but charming, tucked behind a trellis wood fence with clematis and honeysuckle climbing on it. Homey—at least, for his mother. Perhaps he shouldn't take the same casual liberty in his mother's new home as he had in the family home. Heath, his stepfather, probably would bitch about it later, but Aidan shoved the concern from his mind.

"Mon petit. Quelle surprise," the slender brunette greeted, wiping her hands on her apron and rushing to hug him. Aside from their differences in size, age, and facial hair, she could pass for his twin. "J'ai fini de cuisiner le souper. T'en veux-tu?"

"Non," he murmured, declining her dinner offer and planting a kiss on her head. "Chu faitigué."

She stepped away, holding his hands and extending his arms between them. "Mon petit," she repeated. "Tu as l'air différent."

Mom radar. He'd forgotten. His mother always had

the superpower ability of maternal telepathy and read him like a Black Friday sales paper. He attempted to neutralize his face—the equivalent of wrapping his head in tinfoil to block FBI clairvoyant mind control—to deter his mother from questioning him about looking different. No, he refused to be different. He was the same as always, and his recent behavior likely resulted from an extended hangover, and his being upset about Fuselier.

"Aidan," Heath snarled between clenched teeth.

Heath wasn't a bad guy. He held a steady job, didn't drink, and treated Irene well. Aidan couldn't ask for better for his mother. Well, he could, but no one except his dad would ever be good enough for his mother, in his opinion. She'd been desperately lonely after his father's death, lost and isolated. Her friends, all happily married, didn't spare much time for their depressed, widowed friend, unsure of how to continue to include her in their couples' gatherings. Heath had returned the smile to her face. But a jealous streak the depth of Niagara Falls existed in him when it came to sharing Irene with anyone, including her children. And Irene hadn't discouraged it much either.

Butterscotch, the daybreak orange feline, pranced with a sense of entitlement behind Heath; calculatingly focused its ashen eyes on Aidan, and hissed. Aidan hissed in return. Heath, he'd tolerate. The cat, he'd shoot first chance he got. Not literally. Well, maybe. The horrid creature had speared him with its thorny claws and used his shoes for a litter box more times than could be counted. Sometimes, Aidan swore Heath had trained the cat to do it. He'd hoped his mother would develop an allergy and send it to the pound. Truth be told, Aidan wouldn't be broken up if Irene sent Heath to the pound, too. But Heath and the blasted feline came as a package deal. Hoorah, hoorah.

"So, you're eliminated from the nationals," Heath commented, Aidan translating the words into English in an effort to make them sound less harsh. Didn't work. "You should have remained on a Canadian team. Then maybe you'd be playing for the championship."

Aidan grunted. Not going to nationals didn't bother him nearly as much as it should. He'd have more time to heal, to build back the strength in his shoulder. The doctors had released him with a good bill of health, but after each game he needed to ice his shoulder as the soreness crept in faster than usual. Of course, another part of his anatomy ached with soreness, too, but that was a soreness he welcomed—the marvelous sting of feeling Christophe inside him.

"Tu rougis," Irene stated.

Aidan touched his flushed face. "It's hot in here," he replied, masking the truth of his blushing. "C'est chaud," he clarified for her understanding.

In his household, speaking English remained a very sensitive issue. His father had forbidden it completely, going as far as prohibiting any of his children from studying it in school. In that regard, Heath's position paralleled Aidan's father's. Playing on a Canadian team, Aidan had learned some English, mainly how to swear, but the issue hadn't been pushed. However, with the trade, he'd been forced to become an Anglo-Quebecer.

"Oui. *Je comprends*. I've been working on *mon anglais* to converse with you."

Heath snorted, and Aidan interpreted the response as disapproval, which suited him. "That's great. I'll speak to you in English so we can practice."

"Sit."

He pulled out a chair for her and allowed her to sit before seating himself adjacent at the table that had once stood in his family home's formal dining room. Not that his family had been wealthy by any means to have anything formal, but the room had been so dubbed because they only ate there on holidays. Any other time, they ate on the porch, computer desk, couch, or any other place deemed to be convenient.

She patted his fist. "What's wrong? You look sad."

"No, Mom."

"Don't fib to me. You're not happy. It shines in your eyes."

"It's nothing. Post-season melancholy, perhaps."

Her cheeks dimpled. Aidan had the same dimples, but his were hidden by his stubble.

"You should find someone to settle down with, someone who will make you laugh and be happy. When was the last time you went on a date?"

Aidan frowned. "Oh, Mom, you've learned English *too* well."

"I worry. I don't want you to be alone."

Aidan thoughts flew to Christophe. What was he doing? Had he tried to call? Aidan's guilt rose. The flight would be his excuse, although Aidan had turned off his cell long before boarding his plane, and failed to turn it on again upon landing. He hadn't checked messages, texts, or emails. He was engaging in standard blow-off behavior. Christophe deserved better.

Disgusted with himself, Aidan took a deep breath.

"Is it okay that I take the spare room?"

"*Bien sûr.* You never have to ask."

Aidan glanced at Heath. If Heath had understood what his wife said, he would object. Aidan smirked. "Merci."

Unfamiliar with the room layout—it had been unfinished the last time he'd been in it—Aidan couldn't locate the light switch. With his hands outstretched in front of his chest, he shuffled across the carpet until he came to the bed. A noise behind him indicated that Heath had entered without knocking and along with the scruffy cat. He clapped, and the room illuminated. Heath set fresh towels on the dresser.

"You shoot wide too much," Heath stated in Québécois. "You could have won if you had focused more, especially after they put in the backup goalie."

"You're not my coach," Aidan replied in English.

Heath waited for Aidan to translate. When no

translation came, Heath clapped again, shrouding the room in darkness, and exited.

Aidan would apologize tomorrow for his rudeness. Maybe. Or maybe not. But tonight, he only wanted a hot shower and a warm bed. Kicking off his shoes, he padded to the lavatory by following the small sliver of light glowing beneath the door from the hallway but halted when his right foot squished in something wet and slimy. He clapped for the lights and lifted his foot. A string of unsightly globs extended from his foot to the floor. Cat puke!

At the door, Butterscotch, with his toothy grin, licked his paw, his tail thumping lightly against the doorframe.

"Damned cat."

CHAPTER 11

Aidan gently swayed on the porch swing, taking in his surroundings. It was nothing comparable to the view from the old house, and the swing didn't seem to have the same enjoyable movement as previously. It no longer creaked or was positioned the correct distance from the ground. Being much shorter than Aidan and his male siblings, Heath had added links to the chain to lower it to accommodate his height and not theirs. Instead of the swing yielding a feeling of relaxation, it felt imposing. Christophe's shag-carpeted floor had felt more inviting.

He sipped his coffee and scoffed. Decaf. Irene stirred in the kitchen while chatting on the phone with a church companion, boasting into the receiver that her professional hockey player son had come for a visit.

But that was as far as the enjoyment went for both of them. Her pleasure appeared more related to his profession than his visit, and his dissatisfaction grew as she paired him on a blind date with the daughter of her friend. She, his matchmaking mom, wanted him to find happiness with a partner, but she also didn't want him hanging around her home and invading her time with her husband.

And maybe that was how it should be, that at a certain age, a mother was satisfied with a monthly call from her children and no more. Or perhaps, looking at him raised memories of his father. Regardless, he didn't need his mother peddling him off like a flea market bargain. She had plenty of other offspring to give her grandkids to bounce her on knee and make faces at.

Marianna, he heard his mother say, and he cringed. He'd attended school with Marianna Herbert and recalled her vaguely—mainly that she had been a year below him, popular (especially among male students), and been voted "best tits." Aidan had never asked her out, because he'd found her laugh annoying and her friends obnoxious. Over the years, she may have obtained new friends, but he doubted she'd acquired a new laugh.

Irene tapped on the window and asked if he was available for lunch. He easily could have said he had plans and called an old chum for an afternoon of billiards, bowling, or beer at the pub, but decided a lunch date may change his perspective. He nodded, and knew by Irene's expression she was pleased and shocked by his unobjecting compliance.

***

Marianna's breasts were huge, larger than in high school, and filled her knit cardigan to capacity—still a teenage boy's dream. However, her bottle-blonde platinum hair swept in a tasteful updo promoted the image of the successful event planner that she'd become and indicated she'd progressed from boys to men. Her narrow waist fanned into shapely hips and a round bottom—good posts to grasp when riding. Aidan frowned. He should have been more turned on than he was.

She greeted him at the sidewalk café with a hug normally shared between old friends, and flopped into a chair before he could pull it out for her. Plopping her designer handbag on the table, she waved to the waitress and ordered a mineral water and the Cobb salad without the bacon, chicken, egg, cheese, or vinaigrette. Since the waitress was at their table, Aidan ordered a double cheeseburger with the works, steak fries, and a soda, despite not being afforded long as he would have preferred to study the menu. They conversed in Québécois.

"I just came from a business meeting," she explained, "and I'm famished. I'm so happy we could meet for lunch. It's not often I get a sit-down meal. Usually I grab a tofu wrap from the mobile restaurant near my office."

Tofu. Yuck. Deduct a point.

"Sounds like you keep busy. Business must be good."

"It is. It's the wedding season, and I have six this month. Two are really big with over two hundred guests."

"Working so closely with brides must be interesting."

"Most are bitchy and should be grateful anyone would marry them in the first place. They elect to go in debt for yards of useless fabric that they'll wear one time before it takes up space in their closet for a lifetime—or worse, they trash the damn thing and think it's cute."

The waitress brought their drinks, and Marianna returned hers for not being cold enough.

"It's ironic, isn't it?"

"What is?" he questioned.

"Well, this is my busiest time of the year, and it's your slowest. Must be nice to get so much time off and not have to work a full year like everyone else."

Was that an insult?

"It equates to the same, considering the number of hours we put in during the pre- and regular season."

She shrugged. "Doubtful. I think anyone in the entertainment industry has a different interpretation of what normal hours are."

"I'm in the sports industry."

"Same difference."

"No, not really." The words tumbled off his lips flatly.

"How's Lee?"

"Who?"

"Lee. Lee Vaughn. You played hockey with him."

"When we were ten."

"Yeah. How is he?"

"I wouldn't know."

"Pity." She smoothed a lipstick line on her bottom lip. "I thought you two would have kept in touch since you were such good friends."

"No, we weren't."

"But he told everyone how you were best friends and how both of you hung out with all your pro hockey mates. You gave him tickets to all the Owl home games."

Lee had played on his grade four hockey team, and the only reason he'd made the team was because his father had been the coach—and a horrible one at that. But even with the nepotism, Lee's hockey skills were so atrocious that he never became more than a benchwarmer, except the one game when he'd lost his balance and skated headfirst into the referee's nutsack while simultaneously scoring for the opposing team. Aidan couldn't recall ever having talked to Lee other than saying hello or asking for a water.

She tapped her well-manicured nail on the table.

"He showed us pictures of you at the games. Are you sure none of this sounds familiar?"

Oui, something did sound familiar: the definition of a stalker.

"I'm positive."

"Hmm." She sounded doubtful.

"Indeed."

"I suppose it's common to forget friends when you become popular. But then again, you always were popular, weren't you, Aidan? Why didn't you ever ask me out?"

Because I didn't want you and knew you'd work my nerves.

"You had plenty of dates without me adding to the harem."

She laughed that dreadful sound—a cross between a pig rooting for turnips and a horse spotting a snake. "Do women have harems?"

He didn't know, but it was politer than calling them johns. He leaned back in his chair. Perhaps his assessment was a bit harsh. To his knowledge, Marianna had never accepted cash in exchange for sex, but she had received rides, gifts, votes, and grades for her talents on her knees in the second-floor storage room outside the library. Originally, the room had been a science lab. After an incident involving a small fire in an experiment gone wrong that occurred long before his time at the secondary school, the lab had been converted for storage. With its dark tinted windows and isolation from other classrooms, it had been a perfect spot for frisky students with more than scholarly inclinations. Marianna hadn't been the only girl—or boy—to use the room. In fact, Aidan had been there a time or two, and that had been how he'd discovered the world of oral sex. For most students, the encounters had been purely sexual, driven by teenage hormonal urges. But Marianna's encounters always entailed quid pro quo. Aidan knew this to be factual, because she'd bargained with his brother, Ethan, for concert tickets.

Aidan had looked forward to attending the sold-out concert with Ethan. His parents had agreed to allow Aidan to attend with the provision he would be supervised by his older brother. He'd pleaded with Ethan for the ticket, and Ethan had agreed to take Aidan as his plus-one. However, once the venue sold out in less than seventy-two hours, people became desperate for tickets. That was when Marianna had set her sights on Ethan. Aidan wouldn't forget the night Ethan had strolled into their home late, his stride loose and his face content, and slapped him on the shoulder, saying, "Sorry, bro, the pussy's too good." Aidan supposed Marianna had forgotten about that incident.

"You know what I mean. You had a full social calendar."

"I would have made room for you."

The food arrived, and Aidan appreciated an excuse not to talk. Generally, he enjoyed savoring each morsel, but today, he crammed food in his mouth as far as his jaws extended. Marianna didn't take the hint, and pecked at her lettuce.

"This is a nice place," she commented, dabbing the corners of her pink mouth with a napkin. Her lips were wire thin, very unlike Christophe's. "I wonder if they do takeout."

"You don't cook?"

"Heavens no. When you work full-time, who has time for cooking?"

Christophe. And he's damn good at it. He chuckled.

"What's funny?"

"Nothing." He sucked down the remainder of his soda. "I hate to rush, but I have business to attend to."

Her petite features coiled in unflattering angles. "I thought you were on vacation. Your team lost the finals, right?"

"They may have." He stood and dropped enough cash on the table to cover the check.

"Maybe we can do this again when you have more time."

"Sure." *In another century.*

He walked from the café to a nearby park, and strolled around a pond. The last time he'd been there, the area had been under construction, with a sign promising a playground. But something must have changed because wrought-iron benches and metal picnic tables stood on grass where slides and jungle gyms should have.

A pair of lovers holding hands passed him and

paused several feet away. The man whispered into the woman's ear, and she giggled with the fervor of a schoolgirl. Then he pointed to the sky at a cloud, and his lips moved. Aidan supposed they played the game of identifying shapes in the clouds, and looked to where the man had pointed at a billowy puff of white that tapered at one end. The other end split jaggedly down its center.

An alligator. I'll be damned.

Aidan looked back to the couple, embracing in an intimate kiss. Thirty seconds longer, and his looking would be voyeuristic. Shortly after, the man withdrew and departed. After he'd disappeared from view, the woman began sobbing. Feeling obliged to do something, although not sure what, Aidan approached her.

"Excuse me, miss, but are you okay?"

She glanced at him with red eyes, her cheeks wet with tears. "He's not coming back."

"Why, may I ask?"

"I told him I wanted a family. He said he wanted the same, but he had *that* look. Then, he said he had to get back to work and would call me later. I know he won't."

Squeezing her hand, Aidan spoke the first words that made sense. "Have faith."

CHAPTER 12

Aidan entered the television room a little after seven, just in time to witness Heath slap Irene on the rear, pull her into his lap, and plant a solid kiss on her mouth. Her arms draped lazily around his neck in surrender. Upon seeing Aidan standing in the doorway, Irene slipped off her husband's lap and onto the sofa cushion. She smoothed her skirt that had slid high on her thigh, and smiled sweetly. Heath grumbled something incoherent, but it took no genius to comprehend the sentiment.

"*Mon petit*, you're back early."

Considering his date had been at noon and he'd been gone seven hours, their assessment of "early" differed. But seeing how he'd interrupted a game of grab-ass, he understood his mother's position. He glared at Heath, then looked back at his mother's smile.

"I'm leaving."

"Quoi? Mais pourquoi?"

Because. Just because. His abrupt decision to leave startled him as much as it did his mother.

"But you've been here less than a day."

"And longer than I should. This is your life." He walked to the spare bedroom to pack—not that he'd unpacked. Perhaps, subconsciously, he knew he wouldn't stay.

His mother followed.

"Aidan, *s'il te plait*, tell me what's the matter. Do you feel uncomfortable around Heath?"

"It has nothing do with Heath. It's just time for me to go home."

"This is your home."

"No." He threw two T-shirts in the suitcase and zipped it. "I need to get used to mosquitoes anyway. They grow to the size of ping-pong balls in Louisiana."

"Stop." She touched his arm. "What has you so worked up? Is it what those rude reporters are saying? Anyone who knows you knows you could never harm anyone."

So, the broadcast had made its way to Canada, and his mother had heard.

"I don't know me anymore. Maybe I did do it intentionally. I've done so many things lately that I can't explain. Maybe that's one of them."

"You've always had a grasp of who you are. Where does this doubt come from?"

He shrugged. "You're more convinced about that than I am."

"You learned to skate before you walked, and your first word was 'hockey.' There's nothing wrong with knowing what you want in your future, but you can't predict it. It's also acceptable to change your mind. Not everything is controlled—at least, not by us. But we always have choices, even with the things we don't control fully. And sometimes, the best things in life are surprises or the unexplained." She patted his knee.

"*Merci*, Mom."

"You need more than hockey in your life. Finding a nice girl and settling down will make you so much happier. All this flying city to city doesn't provide you with any consistency."

"Maybe I don't want a woman."

"What?" Alarm consumed both her face and voice.

Oh, no. Big mistake. Aidan wasn't about to have *that* conversation with his mother. It wouldn't end without tears, and he couldn't handle his mother's tears. He'd witnessed her cry too much in the past.

"Relationships are complicated. Messy."

"Yes, and they're also very wonderful and fulfilling in a way that no career can be. You can't snuggle next to a career. And a career doesn't give you tender kisses in the morning."

They don't give blowjobs or beard burn, either.

"You should stay. Lucille Tremblay has a niece—"

"I think I've had enough of being fixed up for a while."

"Just because one date doesn't work out doesn't mean you stop trying. Lucille's niece is a dentist and—"

"No, Mom."

"But you need someone, *mon petit*."

Aidan grimaced, knowing his mother wouldn't allow the subject to drop. Once she started, she was tenacious.

"I've already met someone… maybe."

"Really? Who is she? Is it serious?"

"It's complicated."

"You didn't get her pregnant, did you?"

"Oh, Mom," he groaned.

"It's a fair question. Your equipment works, doesn't it?"

No, his mother didn't just go there. "Oh, for heaven's sake!"

"A grandchild would be a good thing."

"No one's pregnant. Now, please, drop this."

"Are you certain?"

"Positive." *Unless the laws of reproduction have changed in the last twenty-four hours.*

"You didn't cheat on her, did you?"

"No—"

"Because your father and I didn't raise you to be a rake."

"It's nothing like that."

"Then what is it? You've been sulky and upset since you arrived, and I know it's more than about hockey.

I'm worried about you."

"I'm fine." *A lie*. He wasn't just lying to his mother, he was lying to himself as a matter of self-preservation. Standing, he planted a quick kiss on the top of her head. "I need to call the airport."

CHAPTER 13

What were the odds of booking two flights riddled with turbulence from takeoff to landing? Aidan's bowels twisted in a way most inconvenient for flying, and he was thankful for the three-hour layover at JFK International. He wandered into one of the airport shops in search of antacids, then to the business class lounge.

No sooner had he eased into a bucket seat and made himself as comfortable as the seat allowed, then he felt the unsettling itch of being watched. At first, he chalked it up to paranoia from a lack of sleep and a lousy flight. But then he heard the beat of heavy footsteps, and looked up to find a broad shadow cast over him.

"Aidan?" Brody Simmons adjusted his baseball cap to allow Aidan a better view of his face. "I thought that was you."

"I thought you'd be in Anaheim."

"I'm on my way, but I had business in New York first. Baby mama drama." He sighed. "You're a very hard man to reach. I've been trying to contact you."

"How's Brandon?"

"That's what I wanted to talk to you about." He motioned to an empty seat. "May I?"

Aidan nodded, and Brody flopped into the chair. "I wanted to apologize."

"For what?"

"Billy and the shit he's been pulling. It's like I told Christophe—"

"Christophe?"

"Yeah, he asked me to meet him before I left Saint Anne. He told me you'd come by the hospital. I'd no idea."

"I didn't mean to intrude—"

"Are you kidding? Seeing you would mean the world to Brandon."

"He's conscious?"

"Of course. He's ep—" Brody paused, and adjusted in his chair. "Christophe didn't tell you? He said he would."

Guilt streaked through Aidan again. "I haven't seen him."

"Hmm," Brody muttered, pressing his mouth in a tight line. "He indicated that you would; otherwise, I wouldn't have discussed anything with him."

The guilt stung Aidan harder. "I'm sure he thought so. It isn't his fault. I've been… unavailable."

"This stays between us."

"*Oui*. No problem."

"It's like I explained to Christophe. Brandon had a seizure on the ice."

Aidan sucked in harshly. "From the fall?"

"More like in reverse. The seizure is why he had the fall. He's epileptic. Was diagnosed when he was in diapers."

Aidan gasped.

"He's always kept it a secret. He figured no team would scout him seriously if they knew, and feared something like this might happen. But he's had the seizures under control for years. I guess the stress of the playoffs and the blackmail got to be too much."

"Blackmail?"

Brody swiveled in the chair to fully face Aidan. "It started about a year ago, shortly after you and I tied up that game."

"I didn't take it out on Brandon."

"I know that; I'm not an idiot. If anyone who has ever thrown a punch on the ice took it personally, there would be no one left." He smirked. "Besides, you punch like a girl."

"A girl that swelled your nose."

"Yeah. Still, it wasn't a big deal. You and I are cool."

"Then, I don't understand."

"After that game, I began receiving hate mail—

general run-of-the-mill stuff: how awful I am, I'm a bad sport, I despise losing, et cetera. Nothing serious, especially since most of it's true." He chuckled. "Some weeks later, they turned weird—pictures of me with horns, or my eyes blacked out. I thought maybe it was a kid, because they seemed immature. But then, one night as I was leaving the arena, a lanky guy approached me in a tirade, screaming that I cost him and the Owls everything, and pulled a gun."

"I remember hearing about that."

"Yeah, well, I'm sure you didn't get the entire story." He checked his watch. "After I jumped him—"

"Wait, you jumped a man pointing a gun at you?"

"The guy was a quack, not to mention a moron. He'd left the store sticker on the gun barrel that said it was a starter pistol. Of course I jumped his ass. I would have beaten him to a pulp, too, had security not pulled me off. That's when he got away and ran like the little bitch he was. Anyway, fast-forward to after the playoff game, and I see my stepbrother, Billy, talking to this jerk. Naturally, I think he's targeting my family, but before I can get to them, I see them shaking hands. I questioned Billy about it, and he blew me off."

Aidan scratched his stubble. "Odd."

"No. Calculating. See, I figured it out when I heard the news report regurgitating about you and me again. I mean, how many scuffles on the ice get rehashed a year later?" He shook his head, disgusted. "Billy always has been jealous of Brandon and me for going pro, because he could never make the cut. He's been leaking stories about me for years—it's the main reason Cindy and I aren't together and are having so many issues. Now he's started on Brandon. He knows word leaking about Brandon's medical condition could destroy Brandon's career. He also knows he can't be associated with the leak. So he hints to the press about you targeting Brandon to draw out this fruitcake to do his dirty bidding."

Aside from Aidan's stomach issues, a headache began developing as he tried to make sense of what Brody conveyed.

"I still don't understand."

"My father, our agent, has done a lot to ensure no one learns about Brandon's diagnosis. Since he played in the league himself, he has plenty of connections with sports physicians, medics, and members of the media to keep everything hushed. But Billy still threatens Brandon on the sly. Only an inside source would know about the seizures. The idiot who pulled the pistol on me blames me for you being traded. Billy decided if he stirred up a story about you targeting Brandon, this fruitcake would take the bait to come to your defense, especially once you denied it publicly. Billy then could feed him Brandon's medical record to give to the media." He shook his head again. "I'm so sorry, Aidan. It was never about you."

"Who is this guy?"

"No clue. But he's Canadian, like you. When I

dropped him in the garage, Canadian coins spilled from his pockets."

"Why haven't I heard any of this before about this guy?"

"The detectives investigating thought releasing details would make him harder to catch. Since they didn't believe you were in danger, they advised me not to say anything."

"So, Brandon's not in a coma?"

"No. He has drop-seizures with paralysis, meaning he goes rigid. That's why you didn't see him convulse. After it passes, he enters a postictal state. Sometimes that lasts for hours."

"But he's still in the hospital."

"For observation and medication monitoring. He's going to be fine. And in a few years, after he's established himself in the league, he'll become a spokesperson and advocate for athletes with seizure disorders. He doesn't want to be limited by a disability." Tearing a corner from an empty food bag discarded on a nearby table, he scribbled a number. "Here's Brandon's cell. He'd be thrilled to hear from you."

Aidan accepted the paper and twirled it in his fingers, relieved and confused by the revelation. The two chatted for a bit longer, until Brody's flight was announced. With the heavy burden of Brandon's injury lifted and a renewed sense of aplomb, Aidan wanted to share his joy of liberation—but with only one person.

A second weight crushed upon his shoulders.

Repositioning in the chair as he continued to await his public aeronautical transit departure, Aidan pondered unorthodox thoughts of unlikely scenarios while he listened to the airport radio pump out the rhythms of a wah-wah guitar indicative of seventies funk music. Christophe would love it and probably promenade around the terminal Risky Business style in defiance of his xennial pedigree. And the irony was, Homeland Security probably would overlook it because Christophe had that effect on people. His infectious eyes. His penetrating stare. His entrancing personality.

A man wearing a wrinkled business suit, crooked tie, and a weary expression entered and sat in the chair across from him. The man fumbled through a satchel while carefully balancing an expresso in the other hand and removed a laptop. He plugged earbuds into the computer and then pecked on the keyboard with the speed of a woodpecker. Aidan reckoned the man must have a hearing issue, because the volume that blared into his ears. Aidan heard every word of the video the man watched.

Aidan parted his lips to ask the man to lower the volume but didn't after reconsidering the man's disheveled state. The man reeked of "bad day" stench. Aidan surely understood those and was sympathetic.

"And now for a bizarre story from Oneida County. Here's Kathy Krant reporting."

"The movie theatre had just opened at Tall Harbor

Outlet Mall in Lee when a man wearing a camouflage cape, coral caftan, green tights, and a fedora drove into the crowded parking lot on a riding lawn mower and jumped off with the engine still running. Armed with multiple handguns, Lee investigators report the man rushed into the outlet and opened fire. Witnesses say the gunman was tackled by mall security at the food court. During the struggle, the gunman shot himself in the foot and buttocks, and a stray bullet caused a nearby sherry and wine display to ignite. No other injuries were reported. According to police, the gunman..."

Aidan had no idea where Lee, New York was located, but he made note not to place it on his vacation list. Then, an epiphany struck him. *Lee? Could it be?* He dialed Lesley, but the call went directly to voicemail.

"Hey, Lesley, this is Aidan. I know this will sound strange, but I need you to contact the police detective who is in charge of investigating the assault on Brody Simmons at the arena. Inform the detective that he should question a man by the name of Lee Vaughn. He lives in Quebec."

CHAPTER 14

Finding his seat, Aidan stowed his carry-on and stifled a yawn; although, he wouldn't sleep. As many times as he'd flown, he should no longer become nervous when the fasten seat belt sign glowed. Once in the air, his nervousness always eased. But this time, it exceeded his usual amount of neurotic angst. Aidan rarely identified his emotional state, but if he had to sum it up in a word, "mess" appropriately described it.

One minute, his life was on track, playing in the playoffs. The next, he was fooling around with his team captain and possibly ruining their friendship. And there was no doubt they'd been friends; in fact, better friends than ones Aidan had known since childhood. His treatment of Christophe made him want to curl into a fetal position and rot. He wouldn't dare begin to explore, or worse, analyze, the inappropriate thoughts he had each time he closed his eyes. His dreams could be packaged and placed on an adult video shelf.

But scarier than his X-rated daydreams was the way their connection went beyond the physical. Christophe got him. Christophe didn't just look at him, but rather, peered into Aidan and scoured the inner sanctum hidden from the general public. Christophe had tapped into a part of Aidan that Aidan hadn't known existed. And a sliver of him didn't want to know about it, either. Ignorance truly was bliss.

He wondered what his father would have said about the situation. He couldn't imagine he'd have approved much. Heath definitely wouldn't approve, but he had no real say in anything as far as Aidan was concerned. Truthfully, no one had a say in it. His siblings all would have viewpoints, and usually vocalized them—their disapproval louder than their approval. His mother... he couldn't predict which way she'd fall. He'd like to think she'd be supportive. Then again, she was hell-bent on him having a traditional family. Sure, he could have confided in her and eliminated the guessing altogether, but why drag her into his emotional chaos when he already may have crashed into a dead-end?

Now that he'd successfully mucked things up, how would he sort them? Was repair even possible? Christophe had every reason to despise him.

And even if he and Christophe did come to some kind of understanding, how would it affect the team?

Would their teammates be weird about it? And what about the coaches and owners? There was no teammate dating policy. He guessed nobody had ever considered it an option. However, he could understand how an owner may view it as potentially being problematic, especially if the relationship went sour. Would that place him in jeopardy of being traded again? And what team would pick him up with his current issues? He had nothing in his contract that would protect him. Even if he had, there were always loopholes. Sad to say, but he'd probably be better off being a recovering heroin addict than in his current personal bedlam. His stomach writhed, contracted, and clenched in balls of apprehension. But at thirty thousand feet in the air—or whatever altitude the pilot had taken him to—there was nothing Aidan could do to resolve the matter. Therefore, he decided to attempt relaxing.

The stewardess offered him a pillow and a blanket. He accepted both, but stared out the window into the blackness. As he finally began dozing, the plane jolted.

"Ladies and gentlemen, this is your captain. We are encountering a bit of turbulence. There's no need for concern."

Fan-fucking-tastic. He watched as the attendants in the galley braced themselves between two lavatories. *Time for relaxation option B.*

Repositioning, Aidan shoved earbuds in and flipped on his monitor, partaking of the inflight amenities. The default setting was a twenty-four-hour sports channel, and Aidan clicked on as the hockey playoff recaps were airing.

"The Wolves fell tonight with a three-one loss to the Polars in the first game of the series. Most are blaming the loss on the absence of Brandon Fuselier, the Wolves' goalie, who has been essential in getting the Wolves to the playoffs. During the regular season, Fuselier had a .927 save rate and twenty-two shutouts. Fuselier was injured while attempting to block a goal shot made by Aidan Lefèvre in the last matchup between the Wolves and the Civets in what turned out to literally be a dog and cat fight for the win. Lefèvre now is amid suspicion for targeting. In addition, Lefèvre's off-the-ice behavior has some questioning if the sage, skilled veteran has not fully recovered from his shoulder injury last season and has turned to using performance-enhancing drugs. Sources close to Lefèvre report that the forward's behavior has been erratic and careless, with noticeable personality changes—"

Too tired to muster the energy to be enraged, Aidan changed the channel to a network designated for cartoons, hoping it would be safe to view with no disconcerting or harrowing content. He settled in his business class, full-flatbed seat to watch purple and green talking monkeys scheme ways to obtain extra bananas from the kooky zookeeper, while the aircraft bumped up and down in whatever was rumbling and shaking it outside.

CHAPTER 15

Aidan returned to his house—and it was indeed a house, not a home—and was thankful to find it void of the media. Brick and mortar constructed houses. Love, laughter, and people made homes.

Abandoning his luggage by the front door, he shuffled into his tiny den, complete with a plush sofa and flat-screen. A milk crate served as an end table, and a dolly the furniture deliverymen had forgotten constituted a coatrack. The cost of relocating from Quebec to Louisiana was astronomical, and Aidan had elected to ship the items he cared for most, which wasn't much, and purchase everything else locally. However, he'd not gotten around to the "everything else." Minimalistic living kept cleaning simple but added nothing to establish a homey environment.

He flopped on the couch, clicked on the television,

and removed his cell, finally prepared to deal with it. He scrolled through the texts first and then the voice messages. Most were inconsequential to him, even if of an important business nature, and he either skimmed or skipped them completely, until coming to the ones left by Christophe.

"Where are you?" Christophe's smooth baritone inquired on the fourth voice message from him, realization and sadness in his tone. There was an extended pause, and his hurt pulsated through the silence. "Well... okay." More silence, then a click.

Like that, a click, and it was done. Aidan hung his head, the bile boiling in his stomach. Clicking on the television, he prayed for a diversion or some divine sign of what he should do.

"*In local news, the annual Skate for Dementia charity event is being held tonight at the Cameron Convention Center. Attendees will have an opportunity to have autographs signed and photographs taken with celebrities, including hockey center and three-time national champion Christophe Fontenot from the Saint Anne Civets, while enjoying a night of ice skating.*"

The team roster photo of Christophe flashed on the screen. His deadpan expression in the photograph gave an intimidating warning to opponents. Little would anyone guess that seconds before the picture had been snapped, Christophe had been horsing around with other team members and brandishing his signature lopsided smile that warmed hearts.

"Also in attendance will be—"

Aidan clicked off the television and checked the time. He didn't have a ticket, but he figured he could crash a party.

***

Crashing 101. Act like you know what you're doing.

Aidan strolled past the snaking line awaiting entry, drawing stares as he cut his way to the front. Two greeters dressed in maroon sports jackets stepped in his path, stopping him. Well, not stopping, but rather, blocking. They were lightweights compared to the defensemen who regularly slammed him against the plexiglass.

"Sir, you'll have to go to the end of the line and wait your turn."

"Lefèvre. Aidan Lefèvre," he introduced, peering over his sunglasses in dapper James Bond fashion. He suppressed a laugh at himself. But if he was to play the part of a person who was supposed to be there, he might as well exhibit his dramatic skills.

The greeters stared, unmoving and uncertain.

Aidan pointed at a Civets poster suspended from the ceiling—an action shot of the team celebrating a victory, with <u>Aidan</u> crowded in the middle of teammates. Christophe's left arm was hooked around his neck, and his right arm extended his stick above his head.

Aidan recalled that victory vividly, and the euphoria captured in the photo came from more than winning. He'd felt a part of something. Accepted. A big part of that was due to Christophe, his <u>welcome</u> and camaraderie. Aidan stared at Christophe's grinning face on the poster. Would Christophe grin when he saw him tonight?

The greeters' eyes flashed as they made the positive identification, and one spoke into a walkie-talkie.

"Sorry, Mr. Lefèvre," one of the greeters apologized, opening a glass door. "We weren't informed VIPs would be using the front doors."

VIP. Aidan snickered. *Nope. Just plain Aidan.*

"I'll show you to where they are setting up. This way."

With each step, Aidan's lungs grew heavy, like when his arms gave out and his bench press spotter allowed the bar to crush his chest—a frequent occurrence when his brothers spotted him and a pretty woman passed.

A promoter saw them coming, and approached with a nervous smile, obviously questioning Aidan's presence.

"Mr. Lefèvre."

Twice in one day, he'd been addressed by that title. No one called him mister, and it rang foreign in his ears.

Christophe's head snapped around from the reporter interviewing him, his face refusing to convey emotion. Was that good? His gaze locked with Aidan's before he refocused on the interviewer.

"I'm embarrassed to admit I was unaware of your participation today," the promoter explained. "Give me a minute, and we'll rectify this situation immediately and have a table ready."

"No worries. I'm here supporting the cause." *Among other things.* "No need to make a fuss."

"Not a fuss." He snapped his fingers, and several assistants scurried to his side. "It'll only take a few moments."

"Sure," Aidan stated, crossing to stand behind the reporter asking Christophe why he chose to be involved in the event.

Mentally, Aidan rolled his eyes. What person would not want to help find a cure for dementia? How uninspired. Why not ask Christophe what his favorite ice cream was, what made his pancakes fluffy, what the tattoo on his right shoulder meant, or why his lips were incredibly soft?

Christophe completed his interview, leaned against the table, and unscrewed the cap to a bottled water. Lifting the bottle to his lips, he drank. His tailored trousers had a sharp crease. *Spiffy.* Aidan stifled a groan.

"What are you doing here?" Christophe asked, his tone even.

Aidan glanced to the bystanders within earshot, and stuffed his hands in his pockets. "Charity."

"I see. I'm sure your contribution will be appreciated.

Every dollar raised helps."

"Christophe—"

"Approximately seven-point-seven million new cases of dementia are diagnosed each year. Nearly fifty million people currently are living with it. That's projected to rise to over seventy-five million in the next couple of years."

"Startling." Aidan closed the gap between them. "Can we talk?"

"Mr. Lefèvre," the promoter interrupted, returning. "We have your table ready. Please follow me."

Aidan looked to the area indicated. In a short amount of time, a rectangular table covered with white linen had been erected at the end of the row. A pack of pens, pitcher of water, and stack of pucks had been arranged. Two men in coveralls hastily worked to stick the poster from the lobby onto the wall.

Holding up his index finger, Aidan replied, "One minute."

A burst of chatter erupted as attendees began filing into the room.

Christophe moved behind his table. "It'll be good for your image." He smiled at the approaching fans.

Class dismissed.

CHAPTER 16

The evening lasted longer than Aidan anticipated—so long, in fact, he thought he'd developed carpal tunnel. But he had to admit, having that many people waiting for his scribble scrabble and mugshot stroked his ego. He enjoyed meeting the people who cheered for him, and wouldn't disappoint anyone by denying his signature due to cramping fingers, even when promoters urged him to take a break. Besides, he knew the event must mean a great deal to Christophe, considering what Christophe had revealed about his grandmother being diagnosed with a disease that robbed people of independence and precious memories. If for no other reason, Aidan had participated for Christophe. Yes, selfishly, he'd attended to snag Christophe's attention, but he'd stayed to lend his voice to Christophe's cause—to help. At the very least, considering his own abominable behavior, he owed Christophe that much.

By the time Aidan signed his last autograph, Christophe had collected his belongings and vacated the convention center. How long Christophe had been gone, Aidan was uncertain. In fact, most all the other athletes had left, too. He checked the time, chewed the inside of his cheek, and contemplated. Nine o'clock wasn't so late, he concluded, at least not for a city like Saint Anne.

Saint Anne wasn't a party mecca like its sister city, New Orleans, but it possessed its own mélange of cultures. A short stroll down Rue Cognac quickly led from colonnaded houses flanked by gardens of jasmine, to frilly double-shotgun houses imprisoned by cast-iron filigree, to neoclassical cathedrals with vast courtyards, to bawdy establishments of sensual delight. The locals referred to it as the little town with the metropolitan attitude. However, with a population of 127,316, "small" as a descriptor was quite misleading—which served as one of the quirks of the town.

Standing on the sidewalk outside the convention center and observing the halo of the downtown area reflected in the night sky, Aidan decided Christophe was in his natural element here, and therefore likely would be gallivanting about and not offended by an unannounced guest—assuming he'd gone home. Knowing Christophe, he very well could be on his way to a midnight tree-hugging ceremony or skinny-dipping with sharks. Anything was a coin toss with him.

Swiping the sweat from his forehead, Aidan crossed to his car, swearing he'd never get used to the Louisiana humidity. If he didn't know better, he'd bet money it was hotter at night than during the day. He jerked off his tie, unbuttoned his collar, rolled up his sleeves, and debated if he should chase the ice-cream truck repetitively playing "Shortenin' Bread" like a stuck jewelry box. *What parent has his child out buying ice cream at this time of night anyway? Probably the same kind that would design men's short-sleeve dress shirts to look moronic with a tie.* But these were issues to ponder some other time.

He drove the winding streets leading to Christophe. During the day, the drive seemed long, but at night it was just eerily black. Few streetlamps lit the way, and bayous lined both sides of the narrow, curvy road that was one pothole away from having drivers become a reptile's fine feast. He clicked his high beams on, and if they illuminated something low to the ground that glowed, he'd surely piss his pants. For sure, this was a story meant for Christophe's memoirs. He could entitle it: How I Attempted to Kill My Teammate Via Vehicular Manslaughter One Humid Night. A little religion might be beneficial, Aidan mused. Damned if these weren't the oddest seventy-two hours he'd ever experienced.

By the time he pulled into Christophe's drive, Aidan

had to get himself together. He sat with the engine off, taking deep breaths for three minutes and debating his decision. Several other cars lined the long drive, parked every which way but straight. Hiking up the driveway, he swore again, uncertain if he did so aloud or beneath his breath. This was fast becoming like a visit to the Mad Hatter. The Hatter had gone mad from sniffing mercury. Aidan wondered what he'd sniffed to possess this many conflicting thoughts and emotions. Could it be the odor of too many sweaty socks in the locker room? He rubbed his eyes, and then pinched the bridge of his nose. By golly, the fatigue was making him loopy.

He rang the bell, and after several minutes, a short, stocky man wearing a fedora opened the door. "Hi, come on in," the man greeted with the personality of a television game show host. Far too perky for after sunset. "I'm Sonny."

Of course, you are. "Aidan."

"Yes, I know. Great shot last game. Bummer it didn't pan out in the end." He swung the door wide. "Come, come. Everyone's in the great room having wine."

Aidan followed *Sunny* into the great room where cool air circulated from multiple cane-blade fans. Several guests lounged and chatted. Aidan knew only a few: Nicco; Ramsey Cline, the Civets' center; Ramsey's wife, Rebecca; and Trey, Christophe's neighbor. Although it wasn't fair to claim he knew Trey, since they'd only been introduced briefly the once. But from the way Trey glared at him in stink-eye fashion, one would swear they had a history. Or perhaps it was more of Aidan's loopy imagination.

"Sit here," a leggy brunette clad in a mini so short it threatened to give a tour of the "Garden of Eden" offered, and scooted to make room for him.

Aidan had no idea legs could be that long, and he followed them from her pumps to her... well, never mind.

"Are you a model?" he asked without thinking.

"Yes." She smiled, extending her henna-tattooed hand. "Natalie Maute." Her voice dipped.

Uh-oh. That was an octave too deep for sheer politeness. She turned her knees to his when he sat.

"Natalie does runway for Vicki Patrick Lingerie," Sonny piped in, handing Aidan a glass of wine. "She recently shot her first commercial for them." He introduced the circle of people gathered around the coffee table.

"What brings you by, Aidan?" Trey demanded, roughly enough that several guests' eyes widened. "Couldn't be because you were in the neighborhood."

"Aidan doesn't need an excuse to visit," Christophe answered from the threshold, a corkscrew in one hand and a platter of hors d'oeuvres in the other. "He likes exploring sometimes."

"Last time I went exploring, I broke my leg," Trey muttered.

Oh, yeah. Aidan wasn't imagining a hostile vibe. It had clutched his neck and was about to suffocate him.

But was that a threat?

"That's because you never look where you're going, Trey," Christophe replied, setting the tray on the table and easing onto the armrest of the sofa. "Hazard of the trade, I suppose. Quarterbacks always look forward and never behind."

Trey popped a cheese square in his mouth. "That's not a bad thing."

"No," agreed Christophe. "Until you're blindsided. But then again, we all are sometimes."

Aidan gulped. Punch taken.

"Your heart's too big, Kit," Sonny interjected. "You let people take advantage." Sonny stole a glance at Aidan. "He really is a big softie."

"But I learn quickly, never repeat the same mistake twice." Christophe bit into a grape.

Ouch.

Trey grinned.

Natalie scooted closer. "So, you're the newbie."

Nicco replied, "Aidan's no virgin."

Aidan choked on his own saliva. What the hell kind of three-ring-circus conversation had he entered? And what exactly did Nicco know?

"Speaking of virgins," George, a distinguished gentleman with graying hair, stated.

"We were?" Rebecca asked.

"I found a premium extra virgin olive oil at the new specialty store on Rue DeCant."

"What dishes have you used it in?" inquired Christophe.

"Oh, we haven't used it on food yet," David responded, clutching George's hand with a squeeze shared between lovers.

The group burst into laughter moments before the true meaning registered for Aidan, and he flushed from his toes to his split ends.

"Oh my," Sonny laughed, "someone's bashful."

"Here, pretty boy." Christophe stood and poured wine into Aidan's more than half-full glass. "We're all frank here."

"I see."

"Pretty boy?" Sonny wiggled his eyebrows and licked his lips. "Yes, he is. Mighty pretty. Delectable."

Say what? Aidan drank more than a generous amount. The sweet tang warmed his chest more than usual for a wine. "This is delicious."

"Thank you," George replied. "It's from my vineyard." He waved his hand. "I know many wineries are going for the twist cap for convenience and buyer preference; but I'm telling you, a quality cork can make the difference between good and outstanding."

Christophe raised his glass. "When I grow up, I want to be just like you, George."

Nicco snorted. "Forget it. You're Peter Pan."

"Don't be rude." Rebecca scowled. "Christophe could never fit into a pair of tights with his muscular thighs. You, on the other hand…."

The group laughed.

"Oh, that's cold," Nicco complained, clutching his

chest and pretending to be wounded. "You're a cruel woman. So, that's how it is, Ramsey?"

"Hey, I don't control my woman."

"All hockey players have massive thighs," Natalie cooed, sliding her hand to the inside of Aidan's. "Since you're new to our group, tell us about yourself."

Aidan shifted uncomfortably. "There's nothing to tell."

"There's always something to tell," Sonny insisted, his eyes bright with curiosity.

"Start with the basics," Natalie continued. "Are you single?"

"Ah, cut to the chase, my darling," George chuckled. "Dice the tater and not peel."

Nicco answered. "He's single and unattached. Been that way all season."

"No one special?" Natalie pried.

"Not really." Aidan answered before his mouth could be censored by his brain.

"Excuse me," Christophe mumbled, heading toward a hallway. "I need to check on Claire."

Merde! *Stupid. Stupid. Stupid.* Why didn't he think? Following would be awkward with everyone watching, but just sitting there weighed him down with helplessness.

Trey announced a need to use the bathroom but headed in the direction of Christophe. Damn, why hadn't Aidan thought to use that excuse? But no, he'd sat there like a wart on a frog's ass.

Natalie's hand moved higher, and he whipped his head around, focusing his attention on her. Her lips were moving, but her words were gibberish in his ears.

"Sorry," he replied. "My English isn't too good." Yes, he still struggled at times with English, but not so much that he didn't understand the international language of seduction.

Nicco and Ramsey swapped leery glances but offered no commentary.

"You don't have to talk, honey."

Now how was he to respond to that? Oh, he knew how he was *supposed* to respond. But why wasn't he? Swirling the wine in his glass, he stared at the waves the liquid made in the fine crystal. He didn't own glassware nearly as nice. Even before he'd relocated, his fine china consisted of gas station refillables and fast food value meal cups. For fancier occasions, he had a few glasses that came with a twenty-eight-piece dining set he'd ordered from the internet shortly after moving into his first apartment. But most of those glasses had broken long ago. How was he to know they weren't dishwasher safe? And why was he focusing on a glass?

Faking a cramp in his side, he stood, twisted, and said, "I think I slept wrong on the plane." And if he'd slept at all on the plane, he was sure that would have been a true statement instead of an outright lie.

Christophe and Trey reentered, toting a dry-erase board, easel, markers, pens, two glass bowls, and a notepad.

"Who's ready for doodle charades?" Christophe asked, erecting the easel. His disposition appeared moderately improved.

"Oh," Natalie cooed, and tugged on Aidan's arm. "Aidan gets to be on my team."

"No, I don't know how to play."

"Don't worry. It's the adult version of Etch A Sketch that no one wants to play but must," George chirped. He grabbed a pen and ripped a sheet of paper from the pad. "I say we do book titles the first round."

"Book titles are too advanced for some of the simpletons in this room." Sonny snickered, stealing a look at Nicco and Trey.

Busy with positioning the dry-erase board, the dig was lost on Trey. However, Nicco heard and responded.

"Sonny, you better be glad this wine has me mellow. Otherwise I'd punch you in your shit."

Rebecca crossed her legs and twisted in her seat. "I don't want to be on the same team with Ramsey, Nicco, Trey, or Christophe."

"But I'm your husband."

"Yeah, and? Y'all get far too competitive. Last time, David ended up with stitches."

"Only because Nicco dropped him," Ramsey rebutted.

"Hey, why you have to toss me in the mix?" Christophe griped.

Rebecca cast a laser stare that could cut glass. "Because it was you who suggested body pressing a person to prove a point."

"Yeah, yeah." Christophe swiped his hand in the air and returned to stabilizing the easel. "Fine. You can be on a team with George, Natalie, Sonny, and Aidan. Dave can be on our team."

What? Did Christophe just toss him away?

Natalie clapped her hands like a baby seal gone rabid. "This will be fun."

Merde. Aidan didn't want to be on a team with Natalie. He didn't want to be on a team, period. He wanted to talk to Christophe… alone. When he sat again, Natalie moved even closer. Any more and she would be sitting in his lap.

George explained the rules, and each person wrote a book title on a square of paper then placed the folded paper in one of the two glass bowls. Aidan felt inadequate, as his mind only could conjure three book titles, two of which were, *Lady Chatterley's Lover* by D.H. Lawrence and *The Selfish Giant* by Oscar Wilde. And wouldn't one have guessed that his entries were the first two picked randomly from the bowl? It would have been a good time for an invisibility portal.

Just as Aidan's face was returning from scarlet to his normal shade, Christophe stood for his turn. A peculiar expression overtook his features before they twisted into a wicked grin. His drawing was no more than stick figures—for the most part—but the positions he drew could have been the abbreviated version of the *Kama Sutra,* and the guesses the extended recommended reading.

"*The Fuck Hump Book*," Nicco shouted enthusiastically, jumping to his feet.

"*Wayment*. Hold up." Christophe stopped drawing. "What the hell, Nicco? That's not a book."

"And 'wayment' is a word?" questioned Ramsey, chuckling at Christophe's pronunciation of "wait a minute."

"Five-point penalty for talking," Sonny chastised Christophe.

"All I said was *what*."

"That's another five. You're trying to help him."

"How is that helping?"

"It's a good guess," Nicco protested, and pointed to the dry-erase board. "Look at that hot mess you've scratched all over the place. What is that supposed to be in the corner? A uterus?"

"It's a state, you moron," Christophe defended.

Ramsey jerked Nicco onto the couch. "Sit your goofy ass down."

"That's another five," Rebecca announced.

The buzzer rang, and Christophe flipped the marker over his shoulder. "Man, y'all are cheating."

"What's the answer?" Ramsey huffed, snatching the scrap of paper. "*Memoirs of a Woman of Pleasure* (*Fanny Hill*) by John Cleveland?"

Nicco slapped his hands on his hips. "Who keeps writing this weird shit?"

Slowly, one by one, they faced Aidan.

"Hoss," George laughed, "I hope you never commit a major crime and have to stand trial. You have guilt written on you from the *rootie* to the *tootie*."

"But isn't it cute, though?" Sonny cooed.

Aidan slouched in his seat, his face burning with fever.

Natalie nestled closer to Aidan. "Well, it sounds like a best-seller to me."

"Naturally," Christophe grumbled, his eyes dimming as he returned to his seat beside Trey. He raised his glass. "Cheers."

CHAPTER 17

Around midnight, the party began to wind down, and Aidan offered to help clean up. Trey declined the offer, but Aidan insisted. Christophe failed to respond one way or the other, and began gathering plates.

The three worked in silence until a small horse trotted into the kitchen and beelined for Aidan, pinning him against the sink and pouncing on him like he was prime rib. Her paws clamped his shoulders, and her corpulent head pushed into Aidan's face, slobber drooling from both sides of her muzzle.

"Oy!"

"How did you get out?" Christophe asked, guiding the dog from Aidan's shoulder and stroking her head. "Sorry. No need to be frightened. She's just saying hello."

"She didn't scare me."

"Really? You look pale," Trey muttered.

"He's Canadian. Besides, everyone looks pale to you." Christophe made a *tsking* sound, and the dog followed him across the room. "I shut her in the game room because she gets overly excited with company. The vet doesn't want her jumping and running yet."

"That's a massive dog."

"Well, it *is* a bullmastiff," Trey sneered. "Not a Chihuahua."

Aidan knew his observation was... well, obvious, and thus lame, but Trey was being a dick. What was his deal?

"She's as gentle as they come." Rubbing both sides of the dog's face, Christophe tilted it. "Hard to believe someone would abuse her."

"She was abused?"

"Yeah." Opening a jar decorated with paw prints, Christophe selected a treat and fed it to Claire. "One Easter, my sister bought a bunny for my niece and needed a place to stash it until that Sunday. I agreed to pick it up from the pet store. The store was hosting an adopt-a-thon, and Claire was one of the dogs featured. They had photos of how she'd been starved to bones and beaten, but her size scared people off from adopting her. There was no way I was leaving without her." He propped his elbows on the counter. "You have any pets?"

"No."

"What about when you were growing up?"

"My stepdad has a…" *fleabag* "…cat."

"You're not a cat person?"

"I don't guess."

"Well, you should consider adopting a dog."

"No, that's okay."

Christophe moved to place the plates Trey had dried into the cabinet. "Too much of a commitment, huh?"

Aidan frowned. "It wouldn't be fair. I'm hardly home."

"That's why you hire sitters and walkers."

"Defeats the purpose of owning a pet, doesn't it?"

"Not at all." Christophe closed the cabinet and glanced around the kitchen. "Looks like everything's done. Thanks, guys."

"It's getting late," Trey announced.

"That's right, you have that thing in the morning with the shoe people. I didn't mean to keep you."

"It's fine." Trey tossed the dish towel onto the counter. "You should head to bed. I know you've been up since early."

"Naw, I'm too keyed up to sleep. I'll probably veg a while in front of the tube."

Perfect. Aidan saw an opening. "Want some company?" Aidan's hopefulness was evidenced in his voice. "I never wound down from the customs search—"

An array of emotions raced across Christophe's face before it returned to neutral. "You left the country?"

131

"Just home."

"You went to Quebec." Christophe emphasized each word.

"*Oui*. Is there a problem?"

Returning to petting Claire, Christophe shrugged. "I have no say in where you go." He clicked his tongue. "Come on, Claire. I feel like a comedy… or at least, slapstick where someone gets a pie in the face."

Okay, apparently confessing going to Quebec wasn't the right thing to say. But why was Christophe upset about him visiting home? What was the big deal?

"I'll grab a couple of brews," Trey announced.

"You should get home and rest. I've dealt with those shoe people. Not pleasant. You're going to need your mind sharp. Lock the door on your way out. Claire and I got this." Christophe padded toward his media room. "And Aidan if he wants to stay," he added as an afterthought.

Christophe's tone set Aidan on edge—not that he wasn't already.

"It's okay?" Aidan asked, double-checking.

"Sure, if that's what you want."

Trey's dark eyes shifted right and then left, dubious about where to focus. Or perhaps it was more reluctance than indecisiveness. Aidan could see the thought bubbles formulating above Trey's scalp, scheming a plausible reason to remain.

Ah! That's it. Finally, the light bulb switched on above Aidan's own head, and he gave Trey another consideration. Helpful neighbor, his foot.

After another minute of observation, Aidan left Trey in the kitchen and followed the sound of television voices to the media room, which resembled a luxury movie theatre with sofas. Christophe sprawled in the corner of one, scrolling the menu guide, with Claire stretched on the floor beside him.

"How was Quebec?" Christophe asked without looking away from the screen. He'd kicked off his shoes and gathered his blond locks into a messy ponytail at his nape.

"The same as usual."

Uncertain of where to sit but wanting to be close, Aidan sat at the opposite end of the sofa.

"You look tired," he stated, guilt building that he was interrupting Christophe's rest.

"My feet hurt. Another five years, I'll be wearing support hose." He smirked, indicating his exaggeration. "Maybe I'll design my own line."

"You'd figure a way to make them bell bottoms."

Christophe wagged his finger. "That's not a bad idea."

"Heaven help me. I was being sarcastic." Aidan's shoulders relaxed. "Want me to rub your feet?"

Christophe's surprised gaze abandoned the screen, and he fumbled with the remote. Quickly, he reined in his shock. "You'd rub my feet?"

"If you want." Aidan would have been shocked, too, by his offer, but he'd long ago given up trying to understand why he couldn't think clearly around Christophe.

Wiggling his toes, Christophe set the remote on the console. "Have at it."

Aidan slid along the cushions and placed Christophe's strong feet in his lap. Blue veins puckered beneath the tanned skin. He didn't know why he'd offered. He'd never given anyone a foot massage. Hell, no one had ever given him one. He didn't like feet. They smelled. Well, except for Christophe's. So, now what was he supposed to do? Fake it?

Lifting Christophe's right foot, Aidan applied pressure and worked his fingers in a circular motion. Christophe twitched and then laughed.

"What?" Aidan inquired.

"I'm ticklish."

"Are you serious?" He scratched the bottom of Christophe's foot.

"Yes," he admitted, drawing his legs toward his chest.

Aidan caught his ankle and traced his hand up Christophe's shin—a shin he found twice as erogenous as Nancy's or whatever her name was. He moved closer and placed a wispy kiss on Christophe's knee.

"Don't."

"Why not? Don't you want me to?"

"Of course I do, but I've explained where I stand. I don't want you regretting anything, feeling like I took advantage of you in a vulnerable state amid your distress regarding Brandon's situation. And by the way, Brandon's injury definitely isn't your fault."

"I know. I ran into Brody at JFK. He explained everything. And he told me you called him. Thank you."

"No need to thank me, pretty boy. I didn't do anything."

"You bothered to contact Brody."

Christophe shifted his eyes to the high-speed car chase on the screen. A late model sedan slammed on brakes and crashed into a guardrail as villains in a stolen SUV evaded the protagonist police driving an unmarked squad car.

"I'm a captain. Captains discuss bad calls." He leaned his head against the cushions. "Watch the movie."

Aidan settled back and sighed as he attempted to absorb himself in the predictable plot of a jewel heist gone wrong with the kidnapping of the daughter of an FBI agent who had twenty-four hours to locate her. On any other night, the movie wouldn't have been enough to hold his attention for more than a few seconds. But having it as an excuse to spend time with Christophe more than compensated for the mediocrity of the ninety-minute low budget film.

At the sound of vociferous snoring, Aidan peered at Christophe, expecting to find him asleep. Instead, the green eyes were focused on him, pupils dilated. The heat of his focused stare scorched into Aidan and robbed him of breath. In the light cast by the screen, Christophe's wide shoulders appeared even broader. Aidan's mind buzzed with excitement.

"Yeah, she does that." Christophe grinned, nodding toward Claire. "Sounds human, doesn't she?"

"More like a tractor."

Christophe stretched and yawned.

"I should let you get to bed."

"But it's not even a school night. Besides, the sequel is next."

"This shitty movie has a sequel?"

Chuckling, Aidan reached for the remote. "Who knew you were a movie critic?" He flipped the channel and stopped on a commercial. "Look. It's Natalie."

Aidan watched as the sultry brunette filled the screen and the camera panned up her legs to her triangular face. Her hair tumbled in bouncy curls around her shoulders.

"She was into you. You two exchange numbers?"

"Why would we do that?"

"Because she's nice, pretty, and out of batteries for her dildo."

Aidan's jaw fell open, and Christophe threw his head back in laughter, waking Claire.

"Have you always blushed easily?"

"I don't blush," he denied, his face growing hotter.

"Damn, it's sexy."

The glint in Christophe's eyes sparked hope in Aidan. However, he kept his yearning in check.

Christophe switched the channel again. "You should call her."

"Who?"

"Natalie."

Aidan began to protest, but stopped. "Sure. Maybe we could double. You can ask out Trey. He's gay, right?"

"You'll have to ask Trey. That's his business."

"Was he your lover?"

Settling for a random channel, Christophe steadied his focus on Aidan. "And what if he was? You've had lovers."

"Why didn't the two of you work?"

"*Assuming*," he stressed, "we were, we have different priorities."

Vague. Aidan grunted. "Maybe his have changed."

"Maybe mine have."

"I... I...." Aidan stumbled for words then helplessly stared at the floor.

"You can tell me, pretty boy." Christophe placed his hand on Aidan's shoulder reassuringly.

"I don't want to be gay."

"So, don't be."

"I don't think it's a matter of choice. I laugh every time I think of you, and weird things happen in my stomach."

Christophe winced. "Is that supposed to be a compliment? Because saying I give you gas sucks."

"I mean the thought of you gives me happy moths."

"I believe the expression is butterflies."

"No. Moths. They chew holes in my intestines when I'm not with you, and flap when I am."

"Um… okay." He grinned.

"I don't know how to do this."

"Start by relaxing." Christophe brushed the hair away from Aidan's forehead. "You drove all the way out here for a reason."

"I've never felt this type of… connection with anyone. The want. Need."

"And that's bad?"

"Honestly?" He wheezed an uneasy breath. "It's terrifying as fuck. All I want to do…." He raised his head and locked gazes with Christophe.

"What do you want to do?"

"This."

Aidan planted both hands on the outside of Christophe's thighs and leaned his long frame forward until their noses touched. He hesitated before progressing, kissing Christophe with roughness and desperation. Christophe withdrew an inch, but Aidan followed, his knees coming onto the sofa and straddling Christophe. His weight advantage pushed Christophe into a vulnerable position on his back, with one of his arms partially pinned. Aidan loomed over him like a predator feline. Well, he was a Civet. Despite the slight retreat, Christophe was receptive to the moist kisses dancing across his mouth, neck, and clavicle, encouraging Aidan.

Aidan's arousal exceeded anything he'd ever known. He no longer cared what that meant. His only concern was that he wanted the man whose arm encircled his waist and whose erection pushed against his ass. Aidan shifted, pressing forcefully into it, adding friction, and simulating penetration. Beneath him, Christophe emitted a sound that provoked Aidan to rip at Christophe's shirt. Buttons flew as the fabric parted, and Aidan's caught the tip of Christophe's nipple between his teeth. He tasted delicious and sweet.

"Oh, damn, don't stop," Christophe urged in Aidan's ear, his tone authoritative and heavy.

Aidan hadn't planned on it. He worked his way out of his shirt, then unbuckled his belt. As he did, Christophe freed his partially pinned arm and flipped Aidan onto his back, obtaining the top position. Damn, he was quick. Aidan had no idea how Christophe worked so fast, but within seconds, he'd tugged off Aidan's pants and boxers as well as his own. When Aidan moved, his cock rubbed against Christophe's, and he thought he'd explode. Reaching between them, Christophe stroked both of their cocks as if one, using their precum as lubrication, and reveled in the sensation of how it felt.

Aidan fixated on their two dicks bumping together inside Christophe's hand. Sensations, both physical and emotional, coursed through him, and he shuddered. An ocean of passion formed a tsunami that flowed from his belly to every pore.

"*Foutre!*" Aidan growled, thrusting his hips.

"I hope that means you like what I'm doing."

Aidan couldn't answer. His voice hitched as he convulsed, his seed shooting onto Christophe's sculpted chest and abs.

"That's my pretty boy. Come for me."

Another long stream shot like a fountain spray, this time bringing Christophe to climax, his voice gurgling, pained, and carnal. Heaving, his head flexed forward, causing his blond locks to slip free and tumble toward his face.

Knowing he'd caused Christophe to lose his sophisticated control delighted Aidan, and he smiled, wanting to view him in that ravenous state again. The thought had him stiffening against Christophe's stomach.

"Again?" Christophe grinned. "You don't waste time, do you?"

Aidan combed his fingers through Christophe's silky mane before drawing him in for a deep kiss that was more than casual. Much more. Geez, what was he doing? He released him.

"I want to be in you," Aidan whispered.

"I don't allow… well, not normally." Christophe lifted himself slightly and stroked Aidan's cheek. "Not unless…."

"Unless what?"

"God, Aidan. That's… intimate." Christophe shook his head, tears welling in his eyes. He blinked them away quickly. "You shouldn't ask me."

"Why?"

"Because."

"That's no answer."

"Because I'm close to falling in love with you, and that will push me off the cliff. Because I can't say no to you; and I know for you, you're just exploring and—"

"*Je t'aime.*"

Christophe froze. "What?" he questioned.

"I love you."

"Are you sure?"

"Very." He'd never said those words to anyone other than his mother. And saying them now was a relief, like he was free of a weighty burden. Yes, he loved this man.

"That's good, because I was lying," he confessed. "I'm already head over heels in love with you. I have been for months." He reached for his pants, crumpled on the floor, retrieved a condom from his wallet, and tore open the corner. Expertly, he rolled it down Aidan's length. "I can't wait to feel you in me."

"Really?"

"Yeah."

Reaching into his wallet again, Christophe removed a packet of lubricant and smeared it across Aidan's cock.

As anxious as Aidan was to have this happen, he was uncertain of the mechanics. Sure, he had some idea, but he didn't want to hurt Christophe. "Don't I need to stand?"

"No, just stay as you are, and put your hands on my waist."

Christophe repositioned and lowered himself onto Aidan. Aidan groaned as he felt his cockhead slowly push past Christophe's tight opening, and Christophe's head flung forward.

"You okay?"

"Yeah," Christophe huffed, biting his lower lip. "Just don't move, yet. You're huge."

The comment engorged Aidan more, and Christophe yelped as he began easing down again, until fully penetrated. He paused before lifting his body a few inches. Absorbed in the bliss, Aidan thrust upward. Christophe grunted so deeply, he didn't sound like himself, and Aidan knew he'd hit a sacred spot. Recognizing the signs of a man on the verge of ecstasy, Aidan wrapped one hand around Christophe's shaft and massaged his balls with the other hand. If there was a moment Aidan wished he could freeze in time, this was it. The oneness with Christophe felt like heaven.

Christophe pushed again, and Aidan stroked faster, covering as much surface with each stroke as possible. The pleasure ran deep, and each tensed, giving in to the rolling spasms that made the rest of the world nonexistent. Christophe shot in creamy ribbons on Aidan's abdomen and chest while Aidan simultaneously discharged like a cannon inside of Christophe.

CHAPTER 18

Aidan awoke alone and stretched. His heart sank, fearing he'd awaken from his amazing dream, until he realized he wasn't in his bed. He rubbed his hand across the mattress next to him and frowned. Cold. He didn't like waking alone, and swung his legs over the side of the bed. At the foot of the bed, a navy robe was draped on a post. Not sure if it was for him or coincidentally placed there, he nevertheless put it on and padded to the kitchen. Christophe, dressed in cargo shorts and a T-shirt, was perched on a stool with a glass of lemonade, swiping a tablet.

"Good afternoon, pretty boy. Hungry?"

"Afternoon? What time is it?"

"Almost one."

"*Merde*! Why didn't you wake me?"

"You were sleeping soundly. I thought you could use the rest." Christophe pushed the tablet aside and sat erect. The angst was obvious in his voice. Of course, Aidan's past record was justification for concern. "Did you have some place to be?"

"No." He shuffled across the room to Christophe's side. "It's bad manners to sleep all day at someone else's home."

"Do you hear me complaining? *Mi casa es su casa.*"

Aidan tugged Christophe's shirt at the neckline and studied the bruised skin at his throat. "Did I do that?"

"Either you, Claire, or it's a case of black plague." His eyes sparkled. "It's been a long time since I've had a love bite, and never one this sexy." Fondly, he touched it, remembering how he'd gotten it from Aidan's complete loss of control, then grazed Aidan's hand still grasping the T-shirt.

Startled, Aidan jerked his hand, and Christophe returned his focus to the tablet.

"Listen, if you didn't mean what you said last night… got carried away in the moment… just say so." His hand trembled as he swiped the screen. "Look, Tanners is having a sale on Egyptian cotton sheets."

Aidan placed his palm over Christophe's, steadying it. "I'm sorry for being an ass. I've a lot to learn about how to be with someone, but I meant every word I said."

"You sure?"

"*Oui.* I want an *us*."

"Okay." Christophe moved to kiss him, but Aidan retreated, covering his mouth with his hand.

"Hold that thought. I need to brush my teeth."

"Your breath isn't bad."

"Coming from a man who regularly smooches a slobbering beast." He glanced at Claire sunbathing outside the glass patio door.

Christophe flashed his endearing grin. "Don't be insulting my dog."

"You have an extra toothbrush?"

"Look in the drawer beneath the sink. And help yourself to anything else you need. I'll fix us some lunch."

"Merci."

"Oh, and Nicco is stopping by later. He left his house keys here last night."

"Guess he didn't go home."

"Well, you know, it's Nicco. He arrived with Kim and left with Tabitha, so there's no telling. And sometimes it's better not to ask."

Aidan made his way to the master bath and decided to take a shower. Normally, he wouldn't impose like that, but he reeked of sweat and sex. Plus, a hot shower would help shake the remaining sleep fog from his brain and allow him time to think. It had been a long time since he'd had a good night's sleep, but the thinking he probably could do without.

He remembered his signing day, how nervous he had been scribbling his name on the contract while surrounded by the most important people in his life and the local media. He'd gussied up in his best suit, and his father had fiddled with the knot in his tie while his mother smoothed a cowlick. In his heart, Aidan had known signing was what he wanted to do, was the right choice for him. But even as he picked up the pen to sign, a piece of him feared the commitment.

He felt it now with Christophe, the same fretfulness he'd felt that day. Only this was different. Hockey was a career; if it hadn't happened, he'd have been content to do something else with his life. But he couldn't envision a world without Christophe. He couldn't be indifferent and move on to something else. And he didn't know how to cope with that. Being with Christophe, being in love with Christophe, meant undeniably accepting something about himself.

He finished his shower and selected a T-shirt and Bermuda shorts from Christophe's closet—or, rather closet boutique. Christophe's fifty-foot walk-in with a mirrored chest island, shoe chambers, and crystal chandelier homed rows of clothes from ceiling to floor. Initially, Aidan had hesitated to select anything, but once inside the closet, he concluded Christophe wouldn't miss a T-shirt and pair of shorts. He would have chosen a pair of jeans, but the two inches and twenty pounds difference between them would make Aidan look like an eighties nerd squeezed into Christophe's jeans. He observed himself in the mirror. Never once had he thought he'd be wearing his *boyfriend's* clothes.

Barefoot, he padded to the kitchen where delicious smells of green onion, sun-dried tomatoes, basil, and garlic wafted through the air. His stomach growled, and he placed his palm on it as if to quiet it.

"I hope you like chicken pasta," Christophe stated, cubing a chicken breast.

"I'm gay."

Christophe froze midchop. "What?"

"I'm gay."

Laying the knife on the chopping block, he turned to fully face Aidan standing on the other side of the island. "Okay…. Um…. And this has what exactly to do with pasta?"

"I figured it out in the shower."

"In the shower?" Christophe smirked. "What we did last night didn't give you a clue?"

"This is new for me. Saying it aloud…."

Christophe rounded the island, stood in front of Aidan, and slipped his arm around his waist. "Hey, I get it. It's a big step. We'll take it slow, at your pace. And the next time you decide to rub one out in the shower, let me know, and I'll help."

"Christophe." Nicco's voice boomed, followed by the slamming of the front door. "Where are you?"

"In the kitchen," Christophe answered, moving away from Aidan. "I've told you not to slam my door, you oaf."

Aidan pulled him back close. "Did he ring the bell?"

"Nope. Never does. He knows I keep the doors

unlocked when I'm home."

"Hey, smells like I can bum a meal— Whoa!" Nicco halted at the kitchen entry with Ryan Hopson at his heels. The two looked back and forth between Christophe and Aidan. "Are we interrupting something?"

"No. I was just saying hello," Aidan replied, then kissed Christophe, his lips lightly dusting before teasing Christophe's apart.

"This isn't slow, pretty boy."

"Do you care?"

"Hell no," Christophe murmured.

Ryan pushed passed Nicco and propped his elbows on the counter. "Aw, aren't y'all the cutest? Got any beer?"

"Shut the fuck up, Ryan," Christophe replied, making a face. "In the fridge, bottom shelf."

Nicco joined Ryan at the bar. "It's about damn time you two hooked up. What's for lunch?"

Christophe strolled around the island and returned to chopping. "I don't recall inviting you, but since you asked so nicely, you'll eat whatever the hell I feed you."

Nicco laughed. "Rude. That's not a show of Southern hospitality."

And just like that, Aidan was out of the closet. He studied his teammates, who did not appear appalled or astonished by the scene they had interrupted. In fact, they appeared accepting and jovial. Would others be as accepting? His fans? His family? Well, of the fans, he had no control; and as long as he helped bring a national championship home to Saint Anne, he doubted they would care about anything else. His family... meh. He supposed he should tell them as opposed to them seeing it in the tabloids. However, this wasn't something one just blurted out in a phone conversation or text message. Lesley had been after him to increase his social media presence. So perhaps he should post a selfie of him and Christophe to his social media page as an announcement.

Naw. "That would be tacky."

"What would?" Nicco inquired.

Realizing he'd spoken aloud, Aidan brought himself back to reality and shook his head. "Nothing." He drummed his fingers on the marble island. "Christophe, how's your passport?"

CHAPTER 19

Aidan disconnected his call with Brandon with a promise to call tomorrow and shoved his phone in his front pocket.

"Are you sure about this?" Christophe questioned, folding shirts into his suitcase.

"You don't want to go?"

"Sure, I do. I'm dying to see all the embarrassing photos of your childhood that every mother keeps and displays when company comes, as well as hearing the equally humiliating stories that go with them—like how you once showed the flamingos at the zoo your pee-pee, because you thought it resembled their beaks."

Aidan's mouth quirked. "You thought your dick looked like a flamingo's beak?"

"Hey, I was three. Gimme a break."

"I can't wait to hear what you did at seven."

"That was my ninja warrior phase. I tried to belly crawl under a barbed wire fence in our pasture as a training exercise. It didn't work out too well."

"And yet, you survived to tell the tale."

Christophe tossed a pouch filled with toiletries in the suitcase's side compartment. "You know there's no going back from this."

"My mom deserves to be told in person. Besides, I left things weird with her."

Zipping the suitcase, Christophe smirked. "You don't think you bringing me unannounced is weird?"

"Well, she already thinks I'm having a breakdown or something. This will solidify her notions." He combed his fingers through his hair. "You don't have to do this."

Christophe clasped Aidan's hand and tugged him close. "Baby, I want to meet your family."

Aidan snapped to attention at the term of endearment, and he tensed for a second. However, he relaxed when Christophe gave him a small squeeze.

"I don't want you to feel rushed or pressured to come out. I'll support whatever you need to do. Maybe you should discuss it with your agent."

Aidan snorted. "She already knows. Hell, she knew before I did. I think everyone may have."

"It doesn't matter as long as you're happy."

Damned if he didn't love this man. "It feels right." Aidan nodded. In fact, nothing had ever felt more right or more perfect. But that didn't make it any less nerve-racking. "But be warned; I don't know how it'll go."

"Expect the same when you meet my family."

Aidan's face twisted. "But I thought your family knew."

"Oh, yeah, they know I'm gay, but—" He smiled, released Aidan's hand, and grabbed the handle of his suitcase. "We can discuss it later. I'm ready."

Aidan inhaled. If only he had the same degree of confidence.

***

The taxi stopped in front of the brownstone, and Aidan hesitated before exiting. He took a deep breath, determined to pretend he didn't feel uncomfortable about the situation and impending conversation.

"You can still change your mind," Christophe whispered.

"No. Let's do this." Before chickening out, he jumped out of the taxi and strolled the short path from the curb to the front door. Under the circumstances, he decided not to go around back and let himself in. He'd behave like a proper guest and ring the bell. He positioned his index finger to press the ringer... and paused. Had he ever used the front door?

"You okay?" Christophe flattened his palm on the center of Aidan's back, something he would have done with any teammate struggling.

"I'm good." Aidan pressed the bell and waited.

The wait seemed long. Seconds passed, then minutes. What was taking so long? Was he once again interrupting an afternoon tryst? Hell, that's where he needed to be—back at the hotel he and Christophe had checked into and dropped off their luggage at before arriving at his mother's home, rolling around between the sheets. Or on top of them. Aidan wasn't picky. They didn't even need a bed. The floor would have sufficed; although, Aidan never had been a fan of carpet burn. But if it meant being with Christophe, he'd make reservations at the burns unit.

Finally, the door swung open, and his mother's mouth transformed from a cheery O to a quizzical one. "Mon petit," she stated, throwing her arms around him. "Why are you out here?" She gave him no time to answer. "Never mind. I'm glad you came back. Where are your bags?"

"At the hotel."

"Hotel? But—" She looked to Christophe, acknowledging him for the first time. A bright light of admiration sparked in her face.

Yes, he is a creature of statuesque, elegant beauty, Aidan mused.

"Come in."

"Who is it?" Heath asked in Québécois.

"Aidan."

"Aidan?" His tone underwritten with antagonism. "He just was here."

Irene led Aidan and Christophe into the living room,

where Heath sat at a card table with a hooded desk lamp, intently working a jigsaw puzzle of a landscape. His jaw tightened, but he failed to lift his eyes from the puzzle. Butterscotch, curled on the sofa, began hissing.

"He's brought a friend."

Heath dragged his stare from the puzzle pieces to Aidan, then Christophe. Recognition registered on Heath's face, and his harsh scowl softened. "Stop that, Butterscotch."

Now that's a first. In all the years he'd known Heath, never once had he heard him scold Butterscotch. Maybe Aidan wouldn't feed Butterscotch to Claire after all.

"Mom, this is Christophe, my… partner." He might as well put it out there. No sense in procrastinating about it now.

"Partner? You mean teammate."

"No, Mom. Partner."

"Aidan, I don't understand."

Turning to Christophe, Aidan flashed him an apologetic glance. "Sorry, but I'm going to need to explain this in Québécois."

"Whatever you need to do," Christophe agreed.

"He's my significant other," Aidan continued in Québécois.

"Your boyfriend?" Irene questioned, tears already seeping from the corners of her eyes.

"But he's a hockey player," Heath stated, scratching his jaw. "You both are."

The comment lay somewhere between a question

and a statement. Aidan pondered how to respond and settled on saying, "*Oui*."

"Is that allowed?"

"I don't think anyone makes etiquette rules for this sort of thing, Heath. And if they do, tough. It is what it is. It's not up for discussion or debate or anything else. I don't give a damn what anyone has to say about it. Christophe and I are together, and nothing about that is going to change."

"Well, then...." Heath stood, approached Christophe, and extended his hand. "It's a pleasure to meet you. Welcome."

Huh? Who is this man? Aidan blinked, and, for a second, he thought his ears deceived him. Here he'd braced for a major opposition from his stepfather, and instead, Heath not only didn't balk, but was welcoming his new lover. Had hell just frozen over?

His mother snatched him into a hug. "Oh, *mon petit*, I'm so happy you've found someone." She released him, then pulled Christophe into a similar hug.

Christophe grinned. "I guess this means she's happy."

"I guess," Aidan replied, stunned. "You're getting more of a reception now than I did when I was called up to the majors."

Christophe grinned. "Well, I am pretty major."

"And I am yours."

THE END

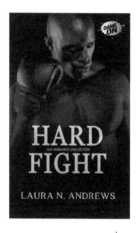
Out and proud Riley Anderson is dancing the night away at a private gay club when he first notices him. Dark, broad, and with muscles to drool over, it turns out he is UFC MMA fighter Craig "The Lion" Johnson. Passion quickly flares and neither can fight the chemistry between them.

After a couple of false starts, Riley and Craig set out to try this thing called dating for real, but clashes are imminent. Too many lifestyle differences make their relationship difficult, but for Riley, it's hard to be kept hidden.

Can he endure being a secret lover? Or will Craig put aside his fears of losing his career and decide what is really worth fighting for?

ACKNOWLEDGMENTS

A motley myriad of people has taken this leap with me to assist in making my dreams a reality. This novel would not be possible without the valuable input, critique, and tireless support of my editors, publisher, cover designer, critique partners, beta readers, and friends. I am truly grateful for having the pleasure of working with each of you and all of the help given in assisting me achieve the next level by being my mentors, teachers, sounding board, cheerleaders, inspirers, confidantes, and shrinks. Thanks to each of you for administering those dosages of tough love.

A very special thank you goes to all who have shared, blogged, read, tweeted, and helped spread the word about my novels. My gratitude is endless. Finally, I thank my family, especially mini-me, for having the faith in me.

ABOUT THE AUTHOR

Genevive Chamblee lives in the bayou country in the deep south where sweet tea, football, good music, and colorful family is gospel. When she is not writing, she can be found attending SEC football games, playing with her dog, sightseeing, or spending time with family.

Genevive writes contemporary romance, erotic romance, fantasy romance, the occult, Creole culture, and southern drama.

Genevive loves to connect with her readers:

WEBSITE: GENEVIVECHAMBLEECONNECT.WORDPRESS.COM
FACEBOOK: FACEBOOK.COM/GENEVIVECHAMBLEECONNECT
TWITTER: TWITTER.COM/DOLYNESAIDSO
GOODREADS: GOODREADS.COM/CREOLE_GIRL
AMAZON: AMAZON.COM/AUTHOR/GENEVIVECHAMBLEE

ABOUT THE PUBLISHER

Hot Tree Publishing opened its doors in 2015 with an aspiration to bring quality fiction to the world of readers. With the initial focus on romance and a wide spread of romance sub-genres, they envision opening up to alternative genres in the near future.

Firmly seated in the industry as a leading editing provider to independent authors and small publishing houses, Hot Tree Publishing is the sister company to Hot Tree Editing, founded in 2012. Having established in-house editing and promotions, plus having a well-respected market presence, Hot Tree Publishing endeavours to be a leader in bringing quality stories to the world of readers.

Interested in discovering more amazing reads brought to you by Hot Tree Publishing or perhaps you're interested in submitting a manuscript and joining the HTPubs family? Either way, head over to the website for information:

WWW.HOTTREEPUBLISHING.COM

CPSIA information can be obtained
at www.ICGtesting.com
Printed in the USA
BVHW080005211221
624507BV00006B/140

9 781925 655407